Say You Love Me

By

Elizabeth Castle

Name: Castle, Elizabeth, author

Title: Say You Love Me

Description: Series: The Heart's Way Book 3

Publisher: In The Air Publishing

Identifiers: ISBN 9781967731169 (ebook) | ISBN 9781967731176 (paperback) | ISBN 9798305574494 (amazon hardcover)

Cover Designer: betibup33

Chapter One

"Please, Selena. I need you to do me this favor."

Selena Powell looked at her nephew, Daniel, and sighed. He was almost six feet tall, so he towered over her quite a bit. He was also so skinny he looked like he never ate, though she knew otherwise. His dark brown hair brushed his shoulders, and this month he was sporting a goatee. Right now his big brown eyes were pleading with her. She hated it when he gave her that puppy dog look. And she really hated it when she knew she was going to cave in. Again. Still, she had to try. "Why don't you hire him?"

"I was going to. I sort of promised him a job." Daniel sent his aunt a pleading look.

"So, again, why don't you hire him?" Selena shoved her strawberry-blonde hair out of her face. She never should have let her stylist talk her into bangs.

"I can't. I sort of got myself into a bit of a financial bind." Daniel quickly held up his hand when he saw his aunt was about to lay into him. "I don't need money. I just need you to give him a job. And I promise he won't be anything like my friend Brian. Carter Sullivan is a man you can rely on."

Selena shuddered. She should refuse to hire the man simply because his name was Carter. Carter was the name of her deceased husband, and she was pretty sure he was one of the lowest forms of life that ever walked the earth.

She wasn't sure she wanted to deal with another one.

"Why is he so desperate to work for you?" Selena asked. Daniel had branched out on his own and had started a talent agency. He employed actors, singers, writers, models, and any other type of entertainment people he could find. He even had clowns, ventriloquists, and mimes on his payroll. Recently he had branched out into catering. He claimed to be able to provide for all of your entertaining needs. He had even sold her his services this past year, though she had other people she usually went with when she took the time to entertain clients. She had to admit he did a good job.

"He was going to head up my new security division. Sometimes the actors and models need a little protection. But I sort of overextended myself on the catering division."

Selena glanced over at Wallace. He had been her bodyguard for the past six years. He also happened to be an excellent hacker. His brain was amazing, not to mention he intimidated anyone who overstepped the clearly marked boundary lines she kept around herself. "All right. Goodness knows I can always use more security around here. What exactly are his job skills?"

Daniel gave her a huge grin. "I'm not completely sure. I do know that once upon a time he was a cop. That was all the recommendation I needed."

Selena shuddered again. Great. His name was not only Carter, but he was an ex-cop. She had had some seriously unpleasant experiences with the local police. But he wouldn't be the first ex-cop on her payroll, and he wouldn't be the last. And it wasn't as if she had to deal with him personally. He'd just be another cog in the wheel of her antiquities business.

"All right. I'll have the paperwork drawn up at human resources. He'll need to come in and fill out an application and all the other necessary documentation. If he's qualified, he's hired."

Daniel stood and bent to kiss his aunt's cheek. "He'll pass all your background checks and will have no problem signing your non-competition clauses, and whatever paperwork you've got lined up to cover your butt."

Selena simply kissed her nephew's cheek back and watched as he waltzed out of her office. She sighed again and dropped down into her seat. She didn't even have to look at Wallace again. He left for the adjoining room where he kept his office, and she knew without asking that he would be running a complete background check on one Carter Sullivan.

An hour later, Wallace came back through the door.

"What's the verdict?" Selena set aside the tablet she'd been reading.

"He passes. He was a cop. Twelve years. He only worked here in the city for the last two years of his career before he quit. He joined the local PD as a detective with the major crime unit. His last assignment involved a sting gone wrong. He quit after being shot multiple times. Permanent damage to his left shoulder, his dominant hand, by the way, and he reportedly walks with a limp. Reports say a punctured lung and damage to his liver. Almost bled to death."

Selena couldn't help but feel a moment of sympathy for him, but first and foremost, she was worried about her company. "Given his injuries, why a security position? Do you think he'll pass our physical?"

"Given what little I can tell from pictures? Yes, he'll pass. And I don't see a limp in the surveillance videos I was able to locate on him. He looks like one tough SOB." Wallace wasn't one to mince words.

"All right. If he passes the physical and is willing to sign all of our contracts, I guess he has a job. Please pass it along."

Wallace nodded and left the room.

Selena picked up her tablet and checked her email. Wallace would have already sent his full report to her. Once she got a good look at the accompanying pictures and videos, she saw what Wallace had seen. It was hard to tell in the pictures, but he had to be six feet at least. He looked to be all lean muscle. His jaw was square, and though it was a tired cliché, he looked like he ate nails for breakfast. There was a small scar on his hairline that went a couple of inches toward his temple on the right side. The best picture Wallace found of him was black and white, but she guessed he had dark brown hair and brown eyes. The five o'clock shadow he sported in the picture gave him a dangerous look. Definitely not a man to mess with.

Selena glanced at the open door. Wallace was tough-looking but in a much more polished way. He had dark hair and dark eyes, but he looked like he belonged on the cover of a men's magazine, or perhaps that was the pages of a women's magazine. He used his looks to attract women and scare off potential threats. She relied on his intimidating looks to counter her softer, more feminine ones. Her greatest wish was to be six inches taller and to not look like she could be a stand-in for a farm girl on *Little House on The Prairie*. The two-thousand-dollar crisp, perfectly tailored suit couldn't mask the freckles sprinkled across her cheeks or the full softness of her mouth. She wanted to look like she was all hard angles and unbendable. Instead, she was only a few inches over five feet, had a lush mouth that her nephew told her men found sexy, and pale blonde hair with a hint of red. If she weren't so vain, she'd have dyed it black. But with her pale, milky skin, the black hair would just make her look washed out. She blew at her bangs. She was going to get even with her stylist. The new bangs made her look vulnerable instead of edgy.

Selena sat back in her chair, her eyes still on the photo of Carter Sullivan. She had to admit he was pretty sexy. The scars didn't detract from what looked like a very healthy male animal. He wasn't handsome, she had to admit. Certainly not in a classical sense. He certainly didn't look like the men she dated. He was hard and lean, whereas the men she dated were usually soft. Her current escort was about twenty pounds overweight and was almost old enough to be her father. But he was soft, and most importantly, harmless. From what she could see, Sullivan was anything but harmless. He looked to be the type of man who took charge and played by his own rules. Definitely not her type.

But as the day progressed, and the rest of the week passed, she found herself thinking about Carter Sullivan at odd times. She'd read the full report Wallace had sent. He was six-one, close to two hundred pounds, and had dark brown hair and dark brown eyes. He had finished high school early and went straight to college. He worked and went to school until he was old enough to enter the police academy. He had a degree in criminal justice. He made detective quickly. He was thirty-five when he voluntarily quit the police department, only two years earlier. Since then he'd worked a few different jobs. He'd worked as a mechanic for six months. He'd worked as a security guard at a bank for three. He worked as a janitor for another three after the bank. Since then there was a gap in his work records. Looked like the ex-detective hadn't worked in a good eight months.

Selena picked up the phone and dialed her nephew. She hadn't asked Daniel how he knew Sullivan, and she was suddenly curious. Unfortunately, Daniel's phone went to voicemail, so her curiosity wouldn't be satisfied yet.

* * *

Carter Sullivan tugged uncomfortably at his tie. When he'd been a detective, he'd worn one often. He just never got used to it. He smoothed back his hair and looked himself over one last time in the mirror. He had no idea what he had just gotten himself into. He'd committed himself to work for Daniel Powell's aunt. Daniel was a nice enough kid, but he was still mostly a kid. Daniel was only twenty-two. Doing security for rich guys' parties or playing bodyguard to an actress or a model once in a while didn't seem like such a bad gig. And he wouldn't have minded going home for a night with said model or actress. The women he used to date had stopped returning his calls once he was no longer a cop. It just proved what he always believed: most women were fickle, and their words of love were not to be believed. He supposed having been a cop made him a bit cynical about the human race, and women in particular. They were quick to play the damsel in distress, and just as quick to stab a man in the back.

Carter had met Daniel when Daniel was working as a waiter at Carter's favorite dive. He'd gotten Daniel out of some hot water when a couple of doped-up teens had come into the restaurant late one night waving knives and threatening the patrons. After Carter had kept Daniel from getting attacked when Daniel had tried to play hero, they'd somehow become friends despite their age difference.

Daniel felt he owed Carter for saving his hide, and Daniel had come up with the brilliant idea of paying him back by promising him a job at his fledgling business. Given the state of his bank account, Carter needed the work and agreed. And because he needed the work, he'd let Daniel pass him off to his aunt. He didn't know Selena Powell, what she looked like, or what she was like, and he didn't much care. But he did know her reputation. There probably weren't too many people who didn't know who she was. She ran one of the largest antiquities businesses in the country, Powell Trading, started by her grandfather years ago. She was a major player in the city he now called home. She was reported to be cold as ice, unscrupulous at the bargaining table, and quite the business shark. She also reportedly went through men like tissues, tossing them out when she was through with them.

Mostly none of that bothered him. He didn't care what

she did or who she did it with. His real problem was he didn't want to be stuck in another job where he had no control or say over how things were done. He'd been in charge more often than not while on the force, and he was the one people went to. He had superiors, but they trusted his judgment in the field. And in the field, you didn't have anyone constantly looking over your shoulder. He'd quit his last few jobs because he was sick of taking orders from people who thought they were somebody because they got to boss an ex-cop around. He also quit because he was tired of taking orders from people more than ten years younger than he was. As soon as he had enough money saved, he was thinking about opening up his own security company. He'd have Daniel be his first client. He knew criminals, and he knew the law. And he knew how to stop people who were determined to wreak havoc on the lives of normal citizens.

Carter pulled on his new uniform jacket and left the house. It still felt odd walking out without his weapon, even after two years. He had a license to carry, but he didn't need it to watch television monitors and escort people in and out of a building. And if he had to guess, Ms. Powell would frown on her staff carrying weapons into her swanky building.

He walked into the headquarters of Powell Trading, once again amazed at how light and bright the building was. The first time he had stepped foot into the building, it had been to sign employment paperwork. The carpet was a deep steel gray, instead of the ugly patterns he saw on the floors of most office buildings. The artwork was tasteful but reproduced.   He found the reproductions amusing, considering the business he was now working for had the real thing in storage. The furniture in the waiting areas looked plush and comfortable. This was a classy operation, he had to admit. He wouldn't mind creating something similar on a smaller scale for his own company one day.

The job he was assigned was pretty straightforward. Some of the couriers who came and went needed to be escorted in and out of the building. He spent the morning following one of the other guards around so he could get the layout of the building and who was where. Not surprisingly, Ms. Powell occupied the top floor of the three-story building. Only people with special clearance were allowed behind those elevator doors. When he wasn't escorting couriers, he was watching security cameras that were placed discreetly behind the reception area. Security in this building was tight, and it ran smoothly. Whoever set it up did a great job. No one came in or went out without getting flagged on the screens.

"How is your first day going?" Daniel opened the door to the security room and saw Carter dutifully monitoring the screens.

"Fine. This is a really cushy gig." Carter couldn't think of anything else to say. He'd been bored for the past hour watching and logging people come and go. He'd rather be back escorting the couriers. Most of them were average men and were nice to chat with.

Daniel leaned casually against the door frame. "Could be worse. You could be my aunt's bodyguard slash assistant. I love her, but she can be a royal pain. I thought I'd come and treat you to lunch. I still feel bad about what happened."

Carter looked at his watch. "My relief should be here any moment. I wouldn't mind going out for lunch and getting some fresh air."

When his relief arrived, Carter followed Daniel out of the building. He did like the kid. Something about him reminded him of himself when he'd been young and not yet jaded. Daniel had an unspoiled easiness about him that spoke to his confidence in his place in the world. Carter knew one day that confidence would be shaken; it was inevitable, but Carter had a feeling Daniel would be stronger for it.

They chatted about sports and world events while they ate. Daniel invited him to a poker game on Friday, which Carter surprised himself by accepting. Carter hated to admit it, but he'd become somewhat of a hermit over the past few months. Besides missing female company, he hadn't gotten together with his buddies at the department because he no longer felt like one of the guys. Turning them down with one lame excuse after another wasn't hard. And since they accepted his lame excuses and finally quit calling, he supposed they felt much the same way. But saying no to the earnestness in Daniel's gaze was more difficult.

They walked back to the office and were about to part company when Daniel's eyes went to the elevator. "Well, well. Coming down to hang out with us regular folk, are you?"

Selena felt an uncharacteristic urge to stick her tongue out at her nephew. Something about him brought out some latent tendencies to behave like a child. Probably because, at twenty-two, he was ten years younger than her. Instead, she gave him a smile, which faded when she saw who he was standing with. She hadn't expected to run into Carter Sullivan, at least not so soon. She went months without seeing the various members of her staff. The company had a few hundred employees, and she only knew a handful of them well.

Carter gave Selena Powell a once over. The first thing he noticed was that she had on ridiculously high heels that, despite their height, couldn't bring them eye to eye. She was probably only five-two to his six-one. The second thing he noticed about her was her incredibly kissable mouth. That mouth could arouse some serious fantasies. She had an almost pixie-like quality to her, but the mouth was that of a siren. The third thing he noticed was her bright blue eyes framed by reddish-blonde bangs and wavy tresses that went just past her shoulders. The overall effect was one of softness and quiet beauty. Her suit was cream-colored, as was the blouse underneath. Nothing about her was flamboyant or over the top. She wore small diamonds in her ears but no other jewelry. She looked delicate. Classy. That was probably the word he was looking for.

Pulling every ounce of professionalism she could muster, Selena held out her freshly manicured hand to Carter. "It's nice to meet you, Mr. Sullivan. My nephew highly recommended you for this job."

Sullivan looked down at the small, delicate hand. He noticed she only wore clear lacquer on her fingers. He took it firmly in his, just barely resisting the urge to squeeze it.

"Nice to meet you as well. But we both know he didn't exactly recommend me for the job."

Selena's blue eyes went icy cold. "I guess we both do know that. But most people would keep that comment to themselves and be happy they have a job."

The ice in her voice gave Carter the sudden urge to take her down a notch. But he bit his tongue and dropped her hand. He glanced over to the very tall, very intimidating man standing slightly behind her, who had taken a step closer at Selena's tone. This would be the hired muscle Daniel mentioned. He almost sneered. "Well, then, I'll just graciously thank you and let you get on your way."

The man gave Carter a warning look. Carter just gave him a bland one back.

"Hey, Wallace, nice to see you." Daniel gave Wallace a wave and watched the pair leave, the other man not saying a word.

"She looked pretty mad." Daniel couldn't help but comment.

"I don't know how to suck up. I'm better at the opposite." Carter clipped his security badge back to his breast pocket.

"She's good at the queen to the peasant routine. But don't let that fool you. She just acts tough. She's really sweet. It only took me five minutes to convince her to hire you. You should practice being cute if you want to get on her good side."

Carter gave him a disbelieving look. "Cute? I don't think I've been able to pull off cute since I was a toddler. Probably not even then."

Daniel chucked him on the shoulder. "No, I suppose not.

You probably intimidated all the other children on the playground. But Selena's not easily intimidated. She'll give back as good as she gets."

Carter nodded at that. He'd never been one to keep his mouth shut or keep his feelings to himself. At least not when they included disgust, disbelief, or disapproval. Selena Powell was the antithesis of everything he stood for. He became a cop because he wanted to help people who couldn't help themselves. People like Selena Powell stepped on those same people he swore to protect. Carter went back to work, praying he could keep this job long enough to save up a nice nest egg before he told her where she could stick her job.

"See you on Friday," Daniel said to Carter; then he winked at the receptionist on his way out.

Carter got back to work.

* * *

The brief confrontation with Carter Sullivan stuck in Selena's mind over the next couple of weeks. She had been able to keep her cool in his presence, but she had felt anything but. She wasn't sure what it was about Sullivan that made her so edgy. Or what it was about him that had her dormant hormones wide awake. She found herself watching for him in the mornings on the security screens she had in her office. She liked to see who was coming and going, and she had been watching for Sullivan more than she wanted to admit.

Even Wallace, who was usually quiet on the subject of

her personal life and habits, had made a couple of comments about her sudden interest in her security guard. And when her latest escort called her to make a date, she turned him down. That in itself should have had warning bells going off in her head. She needed to be seen around town, and having a rich, mostly handsome man escort her was a key component. Her dates eventually broke things off with her, not the other way around. Because it didn't matter who she was going out with, she didn't become attached to any of them. Eventually, they would notice her disinterest, realize they weren't going to talk her into bed, and they would give up and move on. Unfortunately, she was starting to run out of wealthy, influential men to date, so turning the latest one down was a dumb move on her part.

And really, it wasn't as if she could ask Sullivan out. First, he was her employee. Second, he was a nobody. He wasn't a member of the city's movers and shakers. In her business, who you were seen with was important, and she'd spent the last six years devoting herself to her company. Her father might still own half of it in absentia, but he wasn't here to make any of the decisions, and he never would be. And third, Sullivan didn't like her.

And if she were honest with herself, she couldn't fault Sullivan for his immediate dislike of her. She had purposefully cultivated the image of ice queen. She was in a tough business, and it didn't pay to display even the smallest hint of weakness. And rumors were that she used men and tossed them aside. That didn't normally bother her, but having Sullivan look at her with such disdain had been a bit hurtful, though puzzling. But it was the price she had to pay for the life she'd chosen.

Selena opened her laptop and got back to work. She had a line on some artifacts that had been stolen from a local collector. However, since that collector had stolen the artifacts from a Lebanese museum, she felt no remorse in sending what she'd learned about this collector to the proper authorities. She tapped a few more keys, then hit the intercom on her phone. "Wallace."

She released the button and waited. They had been working together for so long that she didn't need to say anything else. She didn't even look up at him when he entered her office. "I need you to take the file I just sent you and forward it anonymously to the proper authorities. Looks like our friend figured out who stole the artifacts from him. He should have them back in his possession in the next day or so. I want them removed from his care before he stashes them away."

Wallace opened the file on the tablet he carried. "Good job. At the rate you're going, you'll be a better hacker than I am."

Selena tried to hide her pleased grin but failed. One of the main reasons she hired Wallace over some of the other applicants was because of his computer skills. Large, intimidating men were easy to come by. She needed a large, intimidating man with investigative and computer skills. Six years ago, she could have prevented what happened had she known how to digitally dig into her husband's life. "I learned from the best. And these artifacts deserve to go home."

Wallace nodded and left.

Selena sighed and leaned back in her seat. She had realized quickly that her antiquities business provided a great opportunity to help governments, including her own, reclaim what was lost. She didn't mind buying and selling antiquities and artifacts, but she strictly followed the laws governing what could and could not be sold. She took pride in following those rules to the letter, and her clients were carefully screened to ensure they held the same beliefs. And it disgusted her that so many artifacts and antiquities were lost to the black market. She knew most of the major players, and she knew, thanks to Wallace's help and teaching, who was honest and who was not. She kept her eyes and ears open and spent a lot of time digging into her client's lives. She had no desire to see priceless artifacts stolen from their rightful owners, stealing the heritage of people who treasured them for their real value, not their monetary one.

Chapter Two

Selena was watching the security cameras when she noticed a man come through her doors that she was sure she had seen earlier in the day. "Wallace, do you know who this is?"

Ellis Wallace watched as Selena tapped a few keys and blew up the image of the man who had just entered the building. "I don't think so."

Selena saved the image and started a facial recognition program. "Have security keep an eye on him."

Ellis, who disliked being called Wallace but allowed it because Selena called most men by their last names, picked up his cell. Despite his dislike, the name had stuck around the office. "This is Wallace. Keep an eye on the visitor in the navy blazer and tan slacks. He's headed toward the elevators."

"What are you thinking?" Ellis glanced over at Selena. She had a solemn look on her face. Normally that wouldn't have bothered him, but he could see anxiety buried underneath it.

Selena tapped a few keys and pulled up an email she had received that morning. "I got another email from that radical group."

Ellis swore. "That's the third one this month. They don't like your methods."

"You mean they don't like my helping countries they consider enemies get their artifacts back." Selena knew many people didn't appreciate the lengths she went to in order to stay within the law. She was outspoken on the rights of all countries to get their heritage back from those who had stolen it. She doubted any of them knew the lengths she went to to make sure they did, which is how she wanted it.

"This particular group has been active lately. They have branches across the U.S. and most of Europe."

Selena saved the email in the file where she kept the other emails. "When European countries were trying to take back what had been stolen from them during various wars, groups like this one were all for it. When you do the same thing for a poor country in Africa or a war-torn country in the Middle East, they call you a traitor."

Ellis pulled up the security footage on another of Selena's screens. Twenty minutes later, the man left. "I'll set up a warning if he returns."

Selena nodded. "And find out who he met with."

An hour later, her secretary buzzed her. "A Mr. Sullivan to see you. He says it's about the man you had security follow."

"Let him in." Selena switched the screens off. It was not uncommon for someone in security to come up to her office. She hadn't known, however, that Carter Sullivan had clearance. She had been ignoring his presence for the past few weeks. Just knowing he was going to set foot in her office had her heart racing.

Carter opened the office door without knocking. Selena

was seated behind a very large, half-round desk. He glanced over to see a complete wall of monitors embedded in the walls. She had on a pale peach suit today; her hair was pulled back in a clip with her bangs framing her face. She looked more like a child sitting behind that desk than the thirty-two-year-old woman she was. He knew because he had done a quick internet search on her the day he met her. Her flawless skin made her look ten years younger.

Selena waved him into the chair and hit the buzzer on her phone. "Who did he meet with?"

Carter saw Wallace enter the room. The faithful guard dog, he thought with disdain. "He met with no one. McCray said to just follow, not intercept."

"And?" Selena's jaw clenched, her impatience showing.

"And nothing. He took the elevator to the second floor. He hit the john, walked down a few hallways, peeked in a few offices, and left. Anyone watching him would think he was looking for someone but didn't find them."

Ellis looked at Carter, then smiled. "But you don't believe that, do you? It must be your cop's eyes. We've yet to get a hit on his name. Footage from earlier today shows him arriving around nine a.m."

"I was escorting couriers this morning, not watching cameras. McCray pulled me in to follow the man." Carter crossed his ankles and leaned negligently in his seat. The thing was so comfy he could take a nap right there.

Selena leaned forward, her spine straight. It wouldn't pay to show even a hint of weakness in front of this man. "I want you to watch the cameras. If he makes another appearance, I want him followed. I want to know if he meets with anyone and what floor he gets off on next time."

"Yes, ma'am." Carter rose and left the room without another word.

"He's got guts; I'll say that for him." Ellis dropped into the chair Carter had vacated.

"How did he get clearance? He's only been here for a month."

Ellis pulled up the email from McCray, who was head of security. "He got clearance last week. According to his supervisors, he's extremely good at his job. He meets with couriers, and he keeps a very detailed log of every conversation he has with them, adding lots of details to his reports others miss. When he monitors the cameras, he catches repeat visitors, noting the date and time of their previous visits. According to McCray, he thinks he should be promoted. Says he's wasted escorting couriers. He'd like him moved to the investigative division."

Selena considered that. She used an outside firm to investigate what she thought of as her other business. Jack Warner, the investigator she worked with, often contacted her when he needed information about people she did business with, met socially, or kept an eye on for herself. In turn, she used his resources to track people who didn't want to be found. Selena hadn't heard from him much since he'd gotten married. His wife, Theo, was very pregnant with their first child already, and they'd been married less than a year. Selena hadn't wanted to bother him. Normally she would send the image of the mystery man to Jack, but she was hesitant to call him for anything less than an emergency.

She didn't use her internal investigators to look into

stolen antiquities or artifacts unless it was part of routine business. She used her internal team to do complete background checks on clients and vendors. She also used them for armed security. The couriers that came and went routinely through the front doors of her building were usually carrying items that were valuable but not dangerous. On the occasions when antiquities came through her back door, items that could get someone hurt or killed, she used her armed security team.

"Do it. But add him to the armed security team, with an appropriate raise in pay and benefits. If he's as observant as McCray says, I'd like him there, at least for the time being."

"Consider it done." Ellis paused at the doorway of his office. "Want me to send the promotion on your letterhead? You might score some points with him if I do."

Selena scowled. "Just do your job."

Ellis laughed, a rare sound coming from him.

* * *

Carter was watching the cameras for their mystery man when McCray came into the security booth. When he returned to his post, a man named Bonner was also there scanning the cameras. Carter was told he was to follow Selena's orders and nothing else for the rest of the week.

"You must have said something right upstairs." McCray clapped him on the back. McCray looked at Bonner, who got the immediate message to leave.

"I can't imagine what that was." Carter kept his eyes on the screen while McCray spoke.

"Ellis Wallace just sent me an email with the paperwork from HR. You've been promoted to our armed security division."

Shocked, Carter's eyes left the screen for a moment before turning right back. "Promoted? Are you sure it doesn't say fired?"

"Your supervisor has been impressed with your work. He told me, and I told Wallace. Looks like he passed that on to Ms. Powell. The email came down from her office telling me to let you know." McCray handed Carter the paper he'd printed out.

Carter glanced down at the paper with Selena's letterhead on it. It was addressed to the head of HR, informing them of the immediate transfer of one Carter Sullivan to the Armed Security Division. His new salary had him choking on his words. He glanced at McCray.

"Ms. Powell believes in paying top dollar for good talent. She could pay me half of what I make now, and I'd still be happy as a clam."

"I'd say Ms. Powell is either easily impressed, or she's turned on by insubordination."

McCray laughed at that. "She's definitely not easily impressed. I'll let you make whatever inferences you like on the other. After your shift, head on up. We'll get you outfitted with a new jacket and a sidearm. You'll have to pass our firearms qualifications, but given your history, I've no doubt you'll pass. And since you were promoted without having taken it first, I'd say Wallace is sure you'll pass too."

"Who makes the decisions around here? Him or Ms. Powell?" It was a serious question. Carter had seen Selena a few times in the past month, and her guard dog was never missing.

"Wallace, no doubt, has a lot of power and sway with Ms. Powell. But don't think for a second she wouldn't fire him, or anyone else, who didn't live up to her expectations. She's been running this company alone for the past six years, and in that time, she has taken it beyond what her father and mother did, or even her grandfather, who founded the company. Her daddy didn't like her interfering in the business when she came on eight years ago, but she pulled his hide out of the fire. He didn't thank her for it. Powell Trading wouldn't be here if it weren't for Ms. Powell. And while she may be strict with employees, firm in her business dealings, and reputedly cold in her personal life, her reputation in this building is sterling. Don't forget that."

Carter nodded. He had come to quickly admire McCray. The man was maybe a year or two younger than he was, but he ran a tight ship as well as any seasoned law enforcement veteran could. He was the one responsible for setting up the top-of-the-line security in this building. He also knew the man wasn't quick with praise or one to gossip and spread rumors. He truly believed Selena was an asset to the company.

Carter cleared his throat, his gaze back on the screens. "So, I just sit and watch for this guy?"

"Those were the lady's orders. She said just for the week. But I'll get you outfitted with your new gear. Ms. Powell has an instinct for people. If she wants this guy followed, it may be that you'll need that gun."

Carter watched McCray leave in his peripherals while

keeping his eyes on the monitor. He had pretty good instincts about people, too. Something about this guy was fishy. He'd give Selena that. Carter had decided to run the company's home-grown facial recognition software on the security footage for the past week. It looked like this guy's first appearance was yesterday, first thing in the morning. Mornings were usually the busiest time of the day, especially for couriers dropping off packages. Most of them arrived early to avoid having the package in their possession any longer than necessary. The guy had shown up again at nine today. Selena must have been monitoring the security cameras herself to notice he'd made a second appearance this afternoon.

The mystery man didn't make a fourth appearance. Once the office was locked up for the day, Carter headed upstairs to find McCray. He was outfitted with a new jacket. This one was black with no logo on it informing guests of who he was. His current jacket was tan with "security" in big letters on the breast pocket.

The weapon he was given was not as powerful as the gun he had at home, the same gun he'd used as a detective. His personal gun was a .40 caliber Smith and Wesson. But the 9-millimeter McCray handed him still packed quite a punch. In the right, or wrong, hands, it could kill just the same.

McCray watched Carter check the gun over before he holstered it. He nodded approvingly. "This locker is yours. You can keep the jacket and weapon here."

Carter clipped his new security badge to the pocket of his slacks before locking up the jacket and gun.

"I'll see you tomorrow," McCray said.

Carter started to follow him out but decided to make a detour. He scanned his new badge and punched in the code to access Selena's floor. The secretary was gone, so he went and knocked on Selena's door.

"Come in, Sullivan."

Carter looked for and saw the discreet camera on the door. He hadn't noticed it earlier, but to be fair, it was well camouflaged, and he hadn't been looking. "I wanted to talk to you."

"If it's about our mystery man, I'm already aware he didn't make another appearance." Selena hit a few keys and shut the screens down.

"I'm beginning to think there isn't much you don't know around here. McCray speaks highly of you, by the way." Carter went and stood at the windows that circled Selena's office. The sun was already setting, and the city's skyline was lighting up.

"You're right. There isn't much I don't know. And McCray speaks highly of me because I speak highly of him. But I'm guessing that's not why you decided to pay me a visit."

"Why?" Carter turned to look at Selena.

"Why what?" Selena wasn't being obtuse.

"The promotion. Why?" It had been bugging him on and off all afternoon. He'd been rude both times he'd come into contact with her.

"I can't believe he did it." Selena rubbed her brow. "Never mind. Let's just say McCray said you were being wasted working front desk security. I trust him, and if he says you should be promoted, then I agree."

"And that's it. He says so, so you do it?"

"Don't get too cocky. He wanted you to join the investigator division. I nixed that idea. You've not been here long enough. Giving you a gun and moving you to the background was the logical place for you, given your work history."

"A gun for hire, is that it?" For some reason, her dismissal of him ticked him off. Normally he didn't let women rile him up, but Selena seemed to have a knack for pushing his buttons.

"In a fashion. According to my sources, you didn't have to quit. You could have remained a cop. One has to ask why, if not for money."

For a moment, Carter saw red. He immediately got himself back under control. His voice was low when he spoke. "You don't know what you're talking about. I suggest you quit while you're ahead."

Selena dipped her head but kept her eyes on his. She had seen his temper flare, and for a moment she had felt fear deep in her belly. She had seen anger like that in the eyes of her father, and then in the eyes of her husband. Selena swallowed down the fear. "I think it's time you left."

"Fine." Carter crossed the room and slammed the door on his way out.

"You're playing with fire." Ellis stepped out from the shadows of the doorway between his and her office.

"Sometimes my impulsiveness gets the better of my common sense." Selena grabbed her purse from her desk drawer and let Wallace lock up behind her.

Ellis's hand went to the small of Selena's back and guided

her out of the building, his body protecting hers. "I see you didn't hit the panic button. You didn't even go for it."

Selena thought about that. "I guess I wasn't really afraid of him. He might lose his temper, but from what I've seen, he has tight control over himself."

Ellis held the car door open for Selena but didn't close it right away. "Any man can be pushed too far. But I think you're right. He has self-control. If I thought otherwise, I'd have been on him in a heartbeat."

Selena leaned back in the passenger seat of her Mercedes. Wallace drove them home in silence. He dropped her off at her front door, made sure the alarm was reset, and left for his residence. He lived in a small cottage on the side of her property. She had built the cottage for him less than a year after he came to work for her when he told her she cramped his style. She took that to mean his girlfriends didn't like him living with her. And she also supposed she hampered his sex life. Who wanted to be intimate when their boss was in the house? The security gate that surrounded her property kept out unwanted visitors, and Wallace had an alarm that would go off should anyone ever get beyond her walls without permission. Their arrangement had worked well for the past six years.

Selena set her purse on the table in the foyer and went to her office. She poured herself a scotch and added ice before kicking off her shoes and lying down on the sofa. Usually she went back to work when she got home, but tonight she had no desire to work. She sighed and took a sip. Her thoughts were on Carter Sullivan. He was a complicated man, and she'd hit a nerve when she mentioned his quitting when he didn't have to. As far as she could tell, the limp he had was barely noticeable, though she had noticed it, and he didn't seem to have any physical limitations from his injuries.

Certainly no limitations that would limit his making love to her, say, on this very sofa. Selena laughed out loud, the sound harsh and unnatural in the quiet of the house. She grabbed a remote, and a hidden television was exposed when the painting that hid it slid into the wall. She flipped on the news. She needed the distraction. Thoughts of Sullivan making love to her had danced their way through her dreams. Again, those dormant hormones seemed to sing whenever Sullivan entered the room. Even his temper was strangely arousing. Now she was imagining the feel of him while she was wide awake. It was embarrassing enough when she woke from dreams of him. It was disconcerting to imagine it while wide awake.

Selena curled up on the sofa, tucking her knees to her chest, trying to stop the unfamiliar ache in her lower body.

Chapter Three

Their mystery man didn't make another appearance. Selena decided it must have been someone's relative or friend. With the threats from the radical group appearing in her inbox regularly, she was becoming paranoid. That Friday night, she sent a notice to McCray that he could begin training Sullivan on his new duties first thing Monday.

That was two weeks ago, and things were back to business as usual. She had a new client due later that afternoon, one that needed her personal attention. She had people who handled most of the day-to-day buying and selling, but when warranted, Selena would come out of her office and mingle with clients. The client had passed the normal background checks, and given the value of the art he wanted to purchase, he had then passed a more rigorous check that she had run personally.

Selena kept busy going over financial statements until Wallace came to get her. She nodded her acknowledgment and finished up what she was reading. She grabbed her badge and tucked it into the interior pocket of her jacket.

Ellis booted up his tablet. It was his habit to do a quick rundown on the way to meet a new client. "Cedric Mallory. Thirty. Unmarried, no children. Owns a yacht club."

Selena laughed lightly at the disbelief in Wallace's voice.

"He owns a very expensive, very lucrative yacht club. And he is looking to buy several very expensive paintings for said club."

Ellis just kept on reading. "Seems to know a lot of the city's lawyers, politicians, and businessmen. I imagine through his club. He passed all the checks."

The elevator opened to the floor below hers. She saw Sullivan standing outside the door. Her heart rate kicked up. He looked amazing in the dark jacket, his black slacks hugging his muscular thighs. Other than a slight nod as he held the door open for them, he made no other acknowledgment of her presence.

Selena waited until the door closed behind them before greeting her client. "Mr. Mallory. I'm Selena Powell. It's very nice to meet you."

Cedric Mallory rose and shook her hand. "I'm looking forward to doing business with you. I hear you have quite the collection of Goodmans."

Selena nodded. She had acquired the Goodman paintings a couple of years ago. The man had been a British artist who had come to the US. When he died of a drug overdose last year, the value of the paintings skyrocketed. And since she owned some of the few not held by private collectors, she could name her price. Mallory had been the first willing to match, and even better, what she was asking for them.

Selena walked to where a large touchscreen monitor hung on the wall. She tapped a screen on her tablet and images of the Goodman paintings appeared. "Once we have a preliminary contract signed, you can see them in person. I had my people authenticate them, but you can bring in an appraiser of your choice to verify them at your convenience."

Mallory scrolled through the images on the screen. "That won't be necessary. Your reputation is such that I think we can forgo the formalities."

Selena nodded and made the appropriate responses, but never had she had a sale of this size pending, and the buyer did not want his own appraisal. Though it was his prerogative, she thought him very foolish.

Wallace kept vigil at the door while Selena and Mallory went through the details of the contract. When they had agreed on the specifics, she emailed the contract to Mallory and her legal team. "Just let me know if you are satisfied with the contract, and we can sign."

Mallory rose. "I'll have my legal team get back to you as soon as they review it."

Selena rose and walked toward the door. "Allow me to escort you out, Mr. Mallory."

"Thank you. I must say I have been impressed by your company, Ms. Powell."

Selena made small talk while they escorted him out. Wallace was at her side, and she noticed Sullivan was following but keeping a discreet distance. When they hit the main lobby and passed the security desk, Selena turned to Mallory to say goodbye. She barely noticed the dark-haired man until he bumped into Mallory. He didn't bother to apologize but kept going.

Selena scowled at the back of the man's head. "Sorry for the man's rudeness."

"No worries, my dear." The man took a step back.

Selena was about to say goodbye when all hell broke loose. She heard a shout from behind her and felt hands shoving her to the floor before Wallace's body landed on top of hers. Several loud cracks that rent the air had her ears ringing. The smack to her head as she hit the floor caused her to see stars.

Selena tried to move, but Wallace's body lay heavy on hers. He wasn't moving. She felt something wet spread on her back and under her belly. She glanced up to see Mallory, his face twisted in rage, as he pointed a gun directly at her. He shouted something at her right before blood spurted from his chest, and he fell to the floor.

"Stay still." Carter pulled his jacket off while shouting orders to the security team nearby.

Selena wasn't sure if Sullivan was talking to her, but she didn't think so. She felt Wallace's weight being rolled off of her. She climbed to her knees, feeling dizzy as she did so.

Carter pulled a knife from his pocket and cut up his jacket. He folded and pressed a large, thick square of cloth into Selena's hands. "Press this over the wound on his chest. Press hard."

Selena didn't understand what Sullivan was saying to her until she looked down at Wallace. A cry tore from her throat. Wallace was bleeding from the bullets he had taken for her.

"Damn it, press." Impatiently Carter tugged Selena closer and forced her hands over the worst of Wallace's wounds.

Selena obeyed, her mind finally registering what had happened. Mallory had pulled a gun on them. Wallace had knocked her out of the way, taking the bullets meant for her. Selena shouted his name. "Wallace!"

His eyes barely opened, but they did enough to focus on her. "Are you hurt?"

Selena shook her head and pressed harder on the wound as blood soaked the cloth.

Ellis looked up at Carter. "Take care of her."

Carter nodded. Ellis's eyes closed once again. He looked over to see tears running down Selena's cheeks. Carter forced himself to look away from her. He shouted more orders to the men who were standing by. When the paramedics arrived, Carter had to pull Selena away from Ellis. He shoved her into McCray's arms, who was standing by. "Hold her."

McCray held onto Selena tightly, who trembled in his arms. "You'd better get seen yourself."

Selena glanced up from where the paramedics were working on Wallace to Sullivan. She saw blood seeping from a wound in his arm. "You were shot."

Carter started to feel dizzy and sat. "Yeah."

"That's all you have to say?" Selena pulled away from McCray and rushed to Sullivan. She shouted to one of the other paramedics.

Carter sat on the floor while the paramedics bound up his arm. "You'll need to ride with me to the hospital."

Selena, who was torn between watching the paramedics as they finally got Wallace on a gurney and on the way to the hospital, and Carter, who was issuing commands from the floor. The paramedic helped Carter to his feet and to the waiting ambulance.

Selena felt an arm steady her when she thought she would fall. She turned to see McCray once again holding her arm. "You need to go to the hospital with Carter and Wallace. Stay with Carter. I'll handle the police here. And have someone look at that cut on your forehead."

Selena followed the paramedics and waited until Carter was strapped to the gurney before she climbed in behind him. She sat completely still as the ambulance raced toward the hospital.

Carter saw how pale Selena was. "Are you hurt?"

Selena, who felt like she was hearing through cotton, looked over at Sullivan. "What?"

"Are you hurt?" Carter tried to sit up, but the strap across his chest prevented him from doing so.

Selena shook her head and immediately realized her mistake. The interior of the ambulance spun around her. She vaguely heard Carter yell at the paramedic who was tending to his arm as she passed out.

* * *

Their mystery man didn't make another appearance. Selena decided it must have been someone's relative or friend. With the threats from the radical group appearing in her inbox regularly, she was becoming paranoid. That Friday night, she sent a notice to McCray that he could begin training Sullivan on his new duties first thing Monday.

That was two weeks ago, and things were back to business as usual. She had a new client due later that afternoon, one that needed her personal attention. She had people who handled most of the day-to-day buying and selling, but when warranted, Selena would come out of her office and mingle with clients. The client had passed the normal background checks, and given the value of the art he wanted to purchase, he had then passed a more rigorous check that she had run personally.

Selena kept busy going over financial statements until Wallace came to get her. She nodded her acknowledgment and finished up what she was reading. She grabbed her badge and tucked it into the interior pocket of her jacket.

Ellis booted up his tablet. It was his habit to do a quick rundown on the way to meet a new client. "Cedric Mallory. Thirty. Unmarried, no children. Owns a yacht club."

Selena laughed lightly at the disbelief in Wallace's voice. "He owns a very expensive, very lucrative yacht club. And he is looking to buy several very expensive paintings for said club."

Ellis just kept on reading. "Seems to know a lot of the city's lawyers, politicians, and businessmen. I imagine through his club. He passed all the checks."

The elevator opened to the floor below hers. She saw Sullivan standing outside the door. Her heart rate kicked up. He looked amazing in the dark jacket, his black slacks hugging his muscular thighs. Other than a slight nod as he held the door open for them, he made no other acknowledgment of her presence.

Selena waited until the door closed behind them before greeting her client. "Mr. Mallory. I'm Selena Powell. It's very nice to meet you."

Cedric Mallory rose and shook her hand. "I'm looking forward to doing business with you. I hear you have quite the collection of Goodmans."

Selena nodded. She had acquired the Goodman paintings a couple of years ago. The man had been a British artist who had come to the US. When he died of a drug overdose last year, the value of the paintings skyrocketed. And since she owned some of the few not held by private collectors, she could name her price. Mallory had been the first willing to match, and even better, what she was asking for them.

Selena walked to where a large touchscreen monitor hung on the wall. She tapped a screen on her tablet and images of the Goodman paintings appeared. "Once we have a preliminary contract signed, you can see them in person. I had my people authenticate them, but you can bring in an appraiser of your choice to verify them at your convenience."

Mallory scrolled through the images on the screen. "That won't be necessary. Your reputation is such that I think we can forgo the formalities."

Selena nodded and made the appropriate responses, but never had she had a sale of this size pending, and the buyer did not want his own appraisal. Though it was his prerogative, she thought him very foolish.

Wallace kept vigil at the door while Selena and Mallory went through the details of the contract. When they had agreed on the specifics, she emailed the contract to Mallory and her legal team. "Just let me know if you are satisfied with the contract, and we can sign."

Mallory rose. "I'll have my legal team get back to you as

soon as they review it."

Selena rose and walked toward the door. "Allow me to escort you out, Mr. Mallory."

"Thank you. I must say I have been impressed by your company, Ms. Powell."

Selena made small talk while they escorted him out. Wallace was at her side, and she noticed Sullivan was following but keeping a discreet distance. When they hit the main lobby and passed the security desk, Selena turned to Mallory to say goodbye. She barely noticed the dark-haired man until he bumped into Mallory. He didn't bother to apologize but kept going.

Selena scowled at the back of the man's head. "Sorry for the man's rudeness."

"No worries, my dear." The man took a step back.

Selena was about to say goodbye when all hell broke loose. She heard a shout from behind her and felt hands shoving her to the floor before Wallace's body landed on top of hers. Several loud cracks that rent the air had her ears ringing. The smack to her head as she hit the floor caused her to see stars.

Selena tried to move, but Wallace's body lay heavy on hers. He wasn't moving. She felt something wet spread on her back and under her belly. She glanced up to see Mallory, his face twisted in rage, as he pointed a gun directly at her. He shouted something at her right before blood spurted from his chest, and he fell to the floor.

"Stay still." Carter pulled his jacket off while shouting orders to the security team nearby.

Selena wasn't sure if Sullivan was talking to her, but she

didn't think so. She felt Wallace's weight being rolled off of her. She climbed to her knees, feeling dizzy as she did so.

Carter pulled a knife from his pocket and cut up his jacket. He folded and pressed a large, thick square of cloth into Selena's hands. "Press this over the wound on his chest. Press hard."

Selena didn't understand what Sullivan was saying to her until she looked down at Wallace. A cry tore from her throat. Wallace was bleeding from the bullets he had taken for her.

"Damn it, press." Impatiently Carter tugged Selena closer and forced her hands over the worst of Wallace's wounds.

Selena obeyed, her mind finally registering what had happened. Mallory had pulled a gun on them. Wallace had knocked her out of the way, taking the bullets meant for her. Selena shouted his name. "Wallace!"

His eyes barely opened, but they did enough to focus on her. "Are you hurt?"

Selena shook her head and pressed harder on the wound as blood soaked the cloth.

Ellis looked up at Carter. "Take care of her."

Carter nodded. Ellis's eyes closed once again. He looked over to see tears running down Selena's cheeks. Carter forced himself to look away from her. He shouted more orders to the men who were standing by. When the paramedics arrived, Carter had to pull Selena away from Ellis. He shoved her into McCray's arms, who was standing by. "Hold her."

McCray held onto Selena tightly, who trembled in his

arms. "You'd better get seen yourself."

Selena glanced up from where the paramedics were working on Wallace to Sullivan. She saw blood seeping from a wound in his arm. "You were shot."

Carter started to feel dizzy and sat. "Yeah."

"That's all you have to say?" Selena pulled away from McCray and rushed to Sullivan. She shouted to one of the other paramedics.

Carter sat on the floor while the paramedics bound up his arm. "You'll need to ride with me to the hospital."

Selena, who was torn between watching the paramedics as they finally got Wallace on a gurney and on the way to the hospital, and Carter, who was issuing commands from the floor. The paramedic helped Carter to his feet and to the waiting ambulance.

Selena felt an arm steady her when she thought she would fall. She turned to see McCray once again holding her arm. "You need to go to the hospital with Carter and Wallace. Stay with Carter. I'll handle the police here. And have someone look at that cut on your forehead."

Selena followed the paramedics and waited until Carter was strapped to the gurney before she climbed in behind him. She sat completely still as the ambulance raced toward the hospital.

Carter saw how pale Selena was. "Are you hurt?"

Selena, who felt like she was hearing through cotton, looked over at Sullivan. "What?"

"Are you hurt?" Carter tried to sit up, but the strap across his chest prevented him from doing so.

Selena shook her head and immediately realized her

mistake. The interior of the ambulance spun around her. She vaguely heard Carter yell at the paramedic who was tending to his arm as she passed out.

* * *

Selena woke on and off during the night, mostly because nurses came in and roused her every hour or so. When she did, Sullivan would open his eyes and watch her be examined. He would wait until she closed her eyes once again before he went back to sleep. It was a little after eight when she finally gave up trying to sleep.

"I'm sorry about yesterday." Selena pulled the covers to her chin and watched Sullivan as he stretched. She knew she was feeling better when the sight of him made her feel a little giddy.   Her headache was still there but felt manageable, as long as she didn't move too much.

"Don't worry about it. You had a rough day." Carter felt the bones in his back pop and sighed. "Hopefully they release you so we can sleep in a real bed tonight."

Selena thought of the very nice, very expensive bed she had at home. Yes, it would be nice to sleep in her bed tonight.

Selena was silent for a while, unsure of what to say or do. Sullivan seemed content to mess with his phone.

Carter broke the silence. "It looks like the shooting made the morning news. Detective Quinlan said he'd try to keep it out of the press as long as possible, but that's impossible. There were reporters outside your building within minutes. News last night said there was a shooting at a prominent place of business and that further details would be released later. Looks like it's later."

"My phone is probably ringing off the hook back at the office. And my cell phone is there, too."

"Probably for the best." Carter picked up the menu to order them breakfast. "What do you want?"

Selena's stomach turned. She thought about a cup of coffee but didn't know if she was allowed. And the thought of food made her queasy. "Nothing."

"You have to eat something, or you'll get sick." Carter picked up the phone and ordered a large breakfast, figuring they could share it. He didn't want to leave her alone to go to the cafeteria.

"I already got sick. I don't want to eat right now." Selena curled up on her side, her back away from Sullivan.

Carter came to sit by Selena. He felt her jerk when his hand touched her back, but she didn't object. Being this close to her, feeling how slender her back was, he realized just how tiny she was. Her personality was so big, and her heels so tall, he had forgotten just how small and vulnerable she was. He kept his touch light, sweeping his hands lightly up and down her back.

"It was my fault." Selena took in a great gulp of air, trying to keep calm. She wanted to cry so badly but didn't want to lose it in front of Sullivan.

"This wasn't your fault. It was Mallory's." Carter continued to try to soothe her.

"I ran the background check. I told Wallace to let me. I didn't find anything that said he might be dangerous."

"Some people are very good at hiding." Carter brushed

the hair back from her face so he could see her eyes as he leaned over her.

"Trust me. Wallace would have. He's the best."

Carter didn't argue with her. Rumors were that Ellis was one of the best computer hackers out there. He might very well have found something Selena missed. "You can't predict crazy. If I learned anything else from my time as a cop, I learned that."

Selena turned her head to look up at him. Her mouth was just inches from his. Why had she never noticed how soft his mouth was? In a harsh face, his mouth looked soft and supple. Her gaze left his mouth and looked up into his dark brown eyes.

A man's voice came from the doorway. "Selena. Thank goodness, you're okay. We saw the news this morning. Theo's been calling hospitals all over town."

Carter pulled his gaze from Selena's to see the couple who had entered the room. The man who had spoken was massive, with dark hair and blue eyes not that different from Selena's. The woman was shorter, though still tall, her honey-blonde hair pulled up into a ponytail. She was also very pregnant.

"Jack." Selena pushed the button on the bed so that she was sitting upright. "Theo."

Jack came over and carefully embraced Selena. They had been friends for a long time. "You should have called me."

Selena held onto Jack for a moment, her fingers digging into his back. "I didn't want to worry you, especially with the baby."

Jack released Selena and stepped back. Theo, Jack's wife,

came and hugged her.

"It's our job to worry. Are you okay? You look pale." Theo brushed back Selena's bangs to get a better look at the bandage.

Selena gave Theo a smile, but it was short lived. "I feel like I ran my head into a brick wall. But otherwise, I'm fine. Wallace is in ICU. He took three bullets. The man who fired is dead."

Jack looked over at the dark-haired man who stood behind Selena. When they'd walked into the room, the man had been bent over her, as if he was going to kiss her. He noticed the sling on his arm. "You must be Carter Sullivan. Word is you're the one who took the shooter out. Took a hit in the arm."

"Yeah, I'm Carter."

"I'm Jack Warner, a friend of Selena's. This is my wife, Theo."

Carter shook Jack's hand, then Theo's. He kept his gaze on the large man. He had to be pushing six and a half feet. When he had hugged Selena, she had held on like she wasn't ever going to let go. He couldn't help but speculate about a relationship between them, despite Jack's very pregnant wife.

Selena rolled onto her back. "The shooter was a client. And your old friend, Detective Quinlan, is on the case."

Jack nodded. "Good. He'll take this seriously. And he'll be used to my interference. I'm going to get in touch with McCray and get whatever is in your files on your so-called client."

"Get the security footage from him. A couple of weeks

ago we had an unknown man enter our building three times. I had him followed but not confronted. Sullivan was keeping an eye out for him, but he never returned. And I did the background check on Cedric Mallory, the client. He passed. Find out how. And I've received more threats from the NAAS."

"The what?" Theo eased herself into a nearby chair. Standing was getting harder and harder with the bulk of her stomach.

"The National Antiquities and Artifacts Society." Jack pushed the recliner button on the chair so Theo could put her feet up. "Selena sent me a few of the emails they sent her. From my investigations, they seemed harmless. No one on the member log raised any red flags."

"As Sullivan was just saying before you arrived, you can't predict crazy. And I don't know for sure they're responsible for the shooting. It seems I was the target."

Jack took Selena's hand and kissed the back of her fingers. "I'll dig further. And I'll dig into this Mallory character. Dead men don't keep secrets."

"Go ahead and contact McCray for what you need, but coordinate through Sullivan. Wallace asked Sullivan to watch over me."

Jack's gaze went back to the man standing quietly to the side. "What's your story, Sullivan?"

"It's Carter. And I'm a retired detective with the city's crime unit. I saw Mallory pull the gun. I shouted, but the man was fast. Had three rounds into Ellis before I could fire."

Jack nodded. "Looks like you were fast enough to warn

Ellis before Selena took the hit."

"She was the target. Ellis got her out of the way. The man was good, but I can't help but wonder why a man would try to murder a woman in the middle of the day in front of several witnesses. And there are armed men all over the building."

Selena spoke softly from the bed. "Not in the lobby. When I think the situation warrants it, I bring certain clients in through the back. The guards in the front don't have guns. There is a gun cabinet in the security room in case of emergency, but the men aren't armed."

Jack rubbed Selena's fingers in his. "What if he knew that? Let's say someone had been scoping out your office and reported back to the gunman. Let's say the man you were keeping an eye out for. Let's say that's how the gunman realized there were no weapons in the lobby. The gunman, who didn't care if anyone saw his face, managed to smuggle in a weapon. He knew he could get a clean shot in the lobby and then quickly exit. In and out."

A new voice spoke from the doorway. "Add a third man to your story."

Theo was the one who spoke. "Detective Quinlan. Nice to see you."

Mac glanced down at Theo. He saw the bulge in her belly. Given the sparks he had witnessed between her and Jack, he wasn't at all surprised. "Congrats."

Jack shook his hand. "Thanks. What third guy?"

Mac answered. "Both Carter and Selena said a man came into the lobby and bumped into Mallory. I'm guessing he passed the weapon to him and then went right through the security checkpoint. Selena said the metal detector is past the lobby. Mallory got in by posing as a high-end client, knew he'd get Selena to walk him out to the lobby where she'd be vulnerable, had the gun passed discreetly to him, and fired at her."

Jack considered that. "He didn't anticipate Carter. He would have known about Ellis, though."

Carter walked closer to the bed. "He could have purposefully fired on Ellis first. Take him out, and that leaves Selena vulnerable to attack. I shot Mallory when he had a gun aimed at Selena's head."

All eyes turned to Carter. Jack spoke. "Now we have to find out why and if it was his idea, or if he was hired."

"That's my job, Jack." Mac knew the man wouldn't listen, but he felt obligated to point it out.

"I'm going to the office and meet with McCray. He's Selena's head of security. I'm going to have him gather any information he has. Why don't you come with me after I drop Theo off at home?"

Resigned, Mac agreed. "I'll meet you there at one. I've got a couple of stops to make."

Selena tried to absorb what the men had said. She had lived through one nightmare and come out stronger for it. She only hoped she was strong enough to make it through this one. "Did you need something, Detective?"

"I came to check Mr. Wallace's condition. He made it through the night. The doctor said he was going to take him off the medication keeping him unconscious later today. He said I could talk to him tomorrow. And I came to see how you were doing."

"I'm feeling better, as long as I don't move." Selena gave him a small smile. He had been very kind to her, much kinder than the police she had met years ago.

Carter didn't like that smile or the way the detective was looking at Selena. "Right now, she needs to rest."

Mac didn't miss the warning in Carter's tone. And he didn't miss the way Selena would watch Carter from the corner of her eye. It was too bad; Selena was quite attractive. In other circumstances, he might have asked her out. Though given the fact she lived in a mansion north of the city, and he lived in a neighborhood that the city liked to call gentrified but was just rundown, he probably would have thought twice about asking her out anyway. And he had a feeling when Selena wasn't knocked down, she would be quite the handful. He felt a slight kick of lust at the thought of taking her on, then pushed it aside. First and foremost, he had a job to do.

"I'll go for now, but I'll be in touch tomorrow. I have the numbers for your landline and cell. I assume you won't be going into the office."

"The landline is unlisted, Detective. I don't have my cell right now, and no, I don't think I'll be back in the office for a few days. I'll have Sullivan tell McCray to cooperate fully."

Mac inclined his head to her, then looked at the rest of them. "I won't tell you to keep your noses out, because I know you won't. But if the man who shot at Selena was not the man who wants her dead, you'd all better keep your eyes and ears open."

Selena waited until the detective had left. "Jack, please take Theo home. And please don't come back. Let John and

Isabelle know I'm fine, and to stay away."

Theo scoffed at that. "Yeah right. We'll be in touch. Just get some rest."

Carter watched as Theo, then Jack, once again hugged Selena and left.

Chapter Four

Carter thanked the worker who brought breakfast and pulled up the tray so Selena could have her pick. "So, who is he really? He's not just an old friend."

Selena eyed the tray, her stomach still queasy. "He is an old friend. He is also an investigator. I work with him on occasion. I haven't seen him much since he got married and his wife got pregnant. They're still in their honeymoon phase."

Carter relaxed a bit. She didn't sound jealous. She sounded happy for him. "What does he investigate? You have your own team of investigators."

"He investigates when I don't want the whole team to know what I'm doing. He also contacts me for information sometimes. I know a lot of influential people."

That was no joke. If the papers were to be believed, she'd dated half of them. "Eat up."

She looked up at Sullivan. "I don't know if I can keep it down. I threw up my lunch yesterday. Detective Quinlan was nice about it, but it was really embarrassing."

Carter saw the scared look on her face, a look that didn't have anything to do with throwing up her breakfast, and he saw the vulnerability she was trying so hard to bury. "Just a bite, then. See if it stays down."

Selena looked at the food he'd ordered. He ordered

scrambled eggs, toast, what looked like it might be bacon, a bowl of fruit, and a cup of yogurt. He was already adding sugar to his coffee. She smiled when he didn't add cream. She didn't either, but she used a lot of sugar.

She looked again and saw the carton of milk. Of everything on the tray, she thought that it might stay down. She opened the carton and grabbed the straw. She took a sip, waited a moment, then took another.

"How about a bite of egg?" He held the fork up to her mouth. She obediently opened her mouth and took a bite of the egg.

"Are you going to the office later with Jack and the detective?" She kept her eyes down, not wanting to see his answer or for him to see the fear in her eyes at being left alone.

"No. McCray is going to come by to bring your purse, phone, and laptop. I'll use your computer to access the files remotely. I can get Jack's number from you." He held out another bite, and she took this one as well.

"Jack will email me what he finds automatically. We've worked together for over six years." She chewed the eggs slowly and took another sip of milk.

"What's the story with you two? You seem close."

Selena knew what he was really asking and didn't see any harm in answering. It might make the two men's working relationship go a little smoother. "I never dated him or slept with him, if that's what you're asking. When we met, it was for a case I hired him for. I can't say we didn't think about it, because we both did. But he's too big, and I'm too small, and somehow or another, we became friends. I was truly happy for him when he met Theo. He lost his first wife, and Theo makes him happy in ways I never could."

Carter held out another bite and didn't protest when she refused it. She had drunk most of the milk and eaten a couple of bites. With the concussion, it was enough. He finished off the rest of the food on the tray.

"Are you involved with anyone?" Selena set the carton down and pushed the tray away when he was finished.

"Why do you ask?" Carter maneuvered the rolling tray to the other side of the room.

"You asked me first. I was just trying to make conversation." And she wanted to know.

"Not since the shooting. It's been a hard transition for me. A woman would just complicate things."

Selena wanted to argue with him, but he probably had a point. Before she had been married, she had been a clingy type of girlfriend. But to be fair, she had been young and desperate for love. She definitely would have complicated his life back then. She couldn't help but feel she might do the same thing to him now. The thought put a damper on asking him any more questions about the women in his life.

She changed the subject. "So, what do we do now? I doubt I'll be able to go home today. And I want to see Wallace when I get released. I need to see him for myself."

"He should be awake by the time you're discharged. And I'll stop in today to see him, as well." What he wanted to ask was if she was involved with Ellis but figured it would just tick her off. She had cried and knelt over the man's body, something he wouldn't have expected from her. She cared about him; that much was obvious. But how much?

Selena slept most of the day. Carter slipped out while she was sleeping and checked on Ellis. The man was awake, and his first question had been about Selena. When Carter assured him she was fine, just a little concussed and tired, the man went back to sleep. He met with McCray, who turned over all of Selena's things from her office. He'd be able to access all her records from her laptop. When he checked her cell phone, he saw multiple calls from Jack and Theo, and a couple of texts from someone name Isabelle. The text said she hoped Selena was feeling better, and to call her as soon as she felt up to it. She also promised not to finish decorating the nursery until she was feeling up to helping, unless the baby came early. He took that to mean Theo's baby.

When he entered Selena's room, her gaze went to his. He saw fear in her eyes that was quickly banked. "I see you're finally awake. You've been asleep for most of the afternoon."

"I thought you left." Selena kept her voice low.

Carter wanted to go to her, kiss that soft mouth, and promise her that things were going to be all right. Instead he said, "I went to see Ellis, and McCray dropped off your things."

"Do you think the man who tried to kill me was the one behind the attack? Or do you think someone else is?"

Carter didn't want to lie to her. "My gut says he was paid. He was just too good. McCray told me about the emails from NAAS. It could be someone who doesn't like your politics."

Selena appreciated his honesty, no matter how much she wished he had said he thought the danger was over. "We're both going to need fresh clothes. Mine are missing."

Carter picked up his phone. "You have a point. Your clothes are considered evidence, and they would be with the police. I can have an old friend of mine bring me some clothes. Who can get yours?"

"Wallace and Jack are the only people who have access to my home. What about my shoes?"

Carter looked up puzzled. "Your what?"

Selena flushed. "My shoes. Do the police have those too?"

Carter was puzzled. The woman probably had a few dozen pairs of shoes, if not more. "I'm guessing yes. What's the big deal?"

"They were a birthday gift from Theo and Isabelle. They said they didn't know what to get me, and that a woman couldn't have enough shoes. They pitched in and spent a fortune on a pair of designer shoes. I want them back." She didn't add that they were the first birthday present she'd gotten since her mom died. And Theo and Isabelle were the only girlfriends she had.

Realizing they were sentimental, Carter didn't make a comment about rich women and how she could find better things to spend her money on than shoes.

"I'm sure you can get your shoes back once they've been processed. I can't guarantee you'll want them back, though, Selena. For now, I'll have my friend grab an extra pair of sweats, socks, and a t-shirt for you to wear."

Thinking about the fact that she had no bra anymore, she asked, "Can I get a sweatshirt instead?"

"Yeah, it's a bit chilly, and you don't have your jacket." Carter sent the text to an old detective friend, told him where to find the key he had hidden, and what to grab. When he got a "no problem," he realized he shouldn't have let his friendship lapse with this particular police buddy.

Selena once again dozed, and Carter met with his friend. He spent the rest of the evening poring over the files Selena had compiled on Cedric Malloy. Everything he saw told him the man was an upstanding member of society. Selena was right; there were no red flags, and the check was extremely thorough. He was impressed that Selena was the one who had put this profile together. There were detectives he knew who weren't this thorough, and it was their job.

There were no hits on the man who had been in the office, and it was possible there was no tie to that man and the shooting. He had to admit Detective Quinlan's supposition that the man was casing the place was a good one. He could very well have been the inside man. Carter knew the man had passed the security check by saying he was the boyfriend of one of the secretaries. He had gained access to the building, but not to secured areas. But he might not have felt he needed to get into the secured areas, just the main part of the building to see how things were laid out.

As for who might have ordered the hit, the NAAS contained a good pool of suspects. Any group could have a few radical members. Or it could be one of Selena's many ex-boyfriends. These men were influential, and maybe one of them didn't like getting dumped. Or it could be any number of rejected clients, current clients, or disgruntled clients. It could simply be because Selena was rich, and therefore a target for some crazy. The possibilities were endless. But the threats she'd received made him lean toward NAAS.

When he'd taken the job with Selena, he hadn't expected to get this involved with her. He didn't want to be this involved with her. But he also couldn't leave her. She had no one she could trust to protect her, so that left him. Ellis asked him to watch her, and he planned to do just that.

"Selena!" A loud voice came from outside the room.

Carter automatically reached for the gun McCray had smuggled in. He quickly tucked it back into his waistband when he saw Daniel's worried face come through the door.

Carter shushed him. Selena was still asleep. He motioned for him to go out into the hall.

"What happened, man? I just saw the news. I tried calling Wallace but got no answer. So I called her friend Jack, and he said Wallace was shot and Selena was in the hospital."

Carter calmed Daniel down and gave him an abbreviated, somewhat sanitized version of the story. No reason to panic the kid. "She'll be fine. I'm going to keep an eye on her until Wallace can."

Daniel's face relaxed. "Then she's got the best. Tell her I came."

Carter couldn't help but shake his head at Daniel's naïve belief and absolute trust that he would take care of his aunt. "I will. Until we figure out why someone tried to kill her, we're asking people to keep away. We don't want you to become a target."

Daniel paled but then straightened his shoulders. "If she

needs me, I'll be there. One more thing, don't let her take any phone calls from my mom. She was all up in arms about how this is why I shouldn't be hanging around Selena. How she's no better than a common thief. Which is probably a better description than the one where she says Selena's nothing more than an exalted antique dealer, and a tacky one at that."

Daniel's mother sounded like his mother's sister, jealous of everyone and everything others had that she didn't. "I'll be sure to screen her calls."

Carter bid Daniel a good night and stood in the doorway of the room, watching Selena sleep. It almost seemed as if there were two different Selena's. There was the cold businesswoman who dated rich men and ran a multi-billion-dollar business. Then there was the other Selena who inspired devotion from her nephew and had friends who seemed like nice, regular people. A month ago he wouldn't have believed there was any depth to Selena Powell. Now he had to figure out which one of her was the real Selena.

* * *

As soon as the discharge papers were signed, Selena was dressed and ready to go. Carter couldn't help but stare. She had on his sweatpants, cinched at the waist, and his sweatshirt. His socks were pooling around her ankles. All in all, she looked like a child wearing her father's clothes. But his thoughts were anything but paternal. He could see the outline of her breasts against the sweatshirt, her nipples beaded against the fabric. He felt a surge of lust, then tamped it down. Her face was bare of makeup, her hair was in tangles, and she was wearing clothes big enough to fit two of her. There shouldn't be anything desirable about her. Yet he couldn't help but notice the smoothness of her skin, and her unconfined breasts swaying against his sweatshirt.

Selena thought Sullivan was staring at her, but then his eyes shifted to the plastic bag the hospital had given her to carry her things in. Sullivan grabbed her bag and then led her to the waiting wheelchair. She had protested that she didn't need one, but Sullivan had told her she would ride in it, or he would carry her. She had no doubt he would embarrass both of them by tossing her over his shoulder. She had relented.

Sullivan wheeled her into the room where Wallace was resting. Selena saw all the machines and tubes Wallace was hooked up to and almost cried out loud. She stood, carefully making her way to his bedside in Sullivan's socks. When she took his hand, his eyes opened.

"Selena." Ellis's voice was soft, but his gaze was steady on hers. "Carter said you were fine, but I wanted to see for myself."

Selena brushed a lock of Wallace's hair back from his forehead. "You saved my life."

Ellis gave her a tired smile. "Carter saved both of our lives. Thank him."

Selena glanced back at Sullivan, who was resting against the wall next to the door. "Yes, I did."

Ellis lifted a hand, brushing aside Selena's bangs to reveal a bandage. "What happened?"

Selena touched her fingertips to the bandage. "Cut my head when I hit the floor. It's nothing."

Ellis's eyes were solemn. "You'll have a scar."

The concern in Wallace's eyes broke her. Tears welled up and she had to cover her face as she began to sob. She bent her head to Wallace's shoulder, hugging him to her as best she could over the railings of his bed. She spoke between sobs. "You could have been killed, and you're worried about a scar."

Ellis looked at Carter. Carter got the message. He came and gathered Selena, pulling her from Ellis, and instead held her against his chest, letting her cling to him as she cried.

"Take her home and keep her there. Get with McCray. Find out who did this." Ellis's energy failed him as he spoke.

"I've been in touch with McCray and the detective on the case. Selena seemed to know him. A Detective Mac Quinlan."

Ellis opened his eyes for a moment. "Good man. Handled a case for Jack and Theo Warner. Friends of Selena's. Call Jack."

"It's been done. Jack is going with Mac to talk to McCray." Carter held Selena to him when she would have pulled away.

"Good. Now get."

Selena fought against Carter, who finally released her. She went to Wallace and kissed him on the mouth. "We'll find out what we can. I'll arrange for someone at the office to stand guard, just in case. Once you're released, I'll bring you home."

Ellis smiled and touched her cheek. "I told you, you

cramp my style."

Selena laughed. "You won't be able to express your style for a little while."

Given how he felt, he knew this to be true. He looked at Carter. "She's yours until I'm back on my feet."

Carter nodded and had to forcefully, but carefully, put Selena back in the wheelchair. His car was in the parking deck, another thanks he owed to his police buddies.

Selena let Sullivan help her into his car. The doctor had warned her she might be overly tired for the next couple of days, and to come back to the hospital if her headaches became worse. Between the tears she'd shed in Wallace's room and the trip through the hospital, her head was aching something fierce. But all she wanted now was to climb into her bed.

Carter punched Selena's address into the GPS and drove sedately to not jostle her. Her eyes were once again closed, her head pillowed in her arms that rested against the door. Her normally healthy skin was dulled, and her normal spunk subdued. Overall, she looked like a woman who had met a challenge head-on and lost.

Carter kept quiet while he drove north. The noise and traffic of the city gave way to open spaces and lots of grass. As he drove through her neighborhood, he couldn't help but notice the impeccable lawns and the huge homes guarded by security fences. As he pulled into the oversized driveway that led to Selena's house, the reality of just how wealthy Selena was came home for him. Her house was stately, the creamy brick adorned with large sparkling windows. The house was two stories and could probably fit four, if not more, of his house inside of it. The driveway was also brick, and the large white fence would keep intruders out. He pulled a sheet of paper out of his pocket that had the security code on it. He punched in the numbers and waited for the gate to open. The mechanism soundlessly opened, allowing just enough room for his vehicle to pass. He stopped and waited for it to close.

He drove up the circular drive and parked in front of the door. He didn't know where she parked her vehicle, but she wasn't going to be in the mood for a walk when he woke her. He got out of the car and looked around. There was a cottage set off to the left of the property, set cozily among the trees. He glanced around her home. He imagined flowers would start blooming soon in the empty beds. Trees sprinkled her lawn, and he could see discreet security cameras hidden inside them. He wondered if the trees had been planted in those locations just for the cameras.

He had Selena's keys, so he opened the door and disabled the alarm. He glanced around the two-story entryway. There was a double staircase right in the middle that led to the second floor. Off to the left of the staircase was a formal living room. To the right was a small sitting room that led to three other rooms that had their doors closed. He imagined one of them was the bathroom. He walked through the sitting room and saw that it led to a formal dining room and a huge eat-in kitchen. When he went back the way he came, he found Selena.

"You should have woken me." Selena had the bag from the hospital in her arms. She closed the door and reset the alarm.

"I was going to, but I wanted to check out the house first."

"I suppose it's what you expected." Selena set the bag down and headed for the staircase.

He was surprised that he didn't expect this house from her. Though it was bigger than he had imagined, what he had seen was nice. The formal living room colors were soft, the furniture was oversized, but it looked like a room he could relax in. He had been expecting something much more formal, colder. "Let me help you up the stairs."

Selena was not too proud to take the arm he offered. "My room is the last room on the left. You can take your pick of any of the other rooms."

Carter kept her steady as he opened the door to her bedroom. It was smaller than he pictured. Or maybe it was the huge bed that stood front and center that made the room look small. He helped her into bed and couldn't help but feel sympathy at the low moan she issued when her head hit the pillow.

"I'll take the room next door. Holler if you need me." Carter left her alone as she quickly drifted back to sleep.

He opened the door next to hers and nodded approvingly. The bed wasn't as large as hers, but it was a queen. He sat down and almost moaned as he sank into the plush mattress, the colors similar to her bedroom. The room even had a private bath. She treated her guests well.

Instead of lying down, he checked out the rest of the upstairs. The house had four bedrooms besides the master, all with their own bath. He went back downstairs and checked out the rest of the house. He raided her fridge, finding beer inside. He wondered if that was Ellis's doing.

He couldn't picture the perfect Ms. Powell drinking beer. The fancy sparkling water inside was more her style.

He peeked into the rest of the rooms. Behind door number one was Selena's office. The desk was similar to the one she had in her work office. Paintings, these not reproductions, hung on the walls. He saw a well-stocked bar and more artwork toward the back of the room, and an oversized couch with several throw pillows. There was even a mini fridge under the bar. He opened a small door and saw a powder room. She could remain in this room for hours and never have to leave.

Door number two revealed a music room and a library. He played a few keys on the piano, then went to examine her bookshelf. There were some very old books on the shelf. And if he had to guess, he'd bet they were very expensive. He saw a cello, a violin, and a couple of guitars hanging on the wall behind the grand piano that took up a good part of the room. Under the window was a bench seat. He couldn't help but wonder if she knew how to play these instruments, or if she'd even read a single one of the books on the shelves.

The third door revealed a huge bath. Though all the guest rooms were upstairs, the bath boasted a soaking tub, a shower, a double vanity, and a separate area for the commode. He couldn't imagine anyone using it, other than an occasional guest who needed to go to the bathroom.

Overall, it was excessive and more than any one person needed. But still, the house did have a nice feel to it. He approved of her color choices, and he approved of the huge television and oversized couch he found at the end of the hall behind the bathroom. Now, this was a room he could enjoy. He found yet another bar, this one fully stocked, and another mini fridge.

Carter kicked off his shoes and stretched out on the couch. He relaxed against a throw pillow and promptly fell asleep.

Chapter Five

For the first couple of days, Selena mostly slept. When awake, she and Sullivan managed to stay mostly out of each other's way. It was hard to believe a week had passed since the shooting. Jack came by each day to check on her and to work with Sullivan to investigate all the different names and angles of who might want her dead. It made Selena shudder to think about it, but she was safe behind the walls of her home.

In a day or two, she and Sullivan would pick up Wallace. The doctor was pleased with his progress and had moved him to a regular room, out of the ICU. Selena had a feeling Wallace would want to recuperate in his own home, so she had already arranged to have a home health nurse stay with him twenty-four hours a day. He would probably be ticked, but he would just have to live with it. And she couldn't help but smile to herself. She'd purposefully hired an older woman, one who wouldn't be charmed by him.

Over the last couple of days, Selena tried to get back into the swing of things. Each morning she woke and pulled on a suit. It made her feel more human, instead of the highly emotional creature she'd been the day she'd cried all over Sullivan. She wasn't that woman anymore; needy, clingy. She could stand on her own two feet, and she would do just that. She might wake up each night because of nightmares, but she wouldn't let them keep her down. Her nightmares were tangled memories of her father, her husband, and the shooting. They jumbled up in her dreams until they drove her from bed at dawn.

She covered the dark circles under her eyes with concealer, put a double layer of anti-aging serum underneath them to keep the puffiness at bay, and acted as if she didn't have a care in the world. She fixed her hair each day, was a little dismayed that she would indeed have a scar on her forehead, then put on her earrings and a pair of high-heeled shoes. She then headed straight for the kitchen, where she forced herself to eat some whole grain toast and drink a cup of coffee before heading to her office.

Sullivan would come downstairs about an hour after she did. She would hear him in the kitchen, where she knew he'd make nothing more than coffee. The first morning he was in her home, she had gone to the kitchen to fix a second cup of coffee and she'd found him in her kitchen propped up against the counter while he waited for her one-cup coffee maker to brew his coffee. It was almost amusing the way his eyes were half glazed. She learned quickly that he was not a morning person. He would do nothing more than grunt at her until he'd poured the first cup down his throat. He would already have his second cup brewing while he finished the first. It was quite the opposite of what she had seen of him in the hospital. There he'd been alert and awake. She figured that here he didn't have to be either of those things first thing in the morning, so he reverted back to his normal behavior.

After his second morning in her home, she avoided him

until he settled himself in what she thought of as the den. It was the only room in the house besides her office that had a television in it, and he would drink his second cup while watching the news. The first morning, she had inquired about what he was planning to do, but the question had gone unanswered when her front door opened. Only Wallace and Jack had access to her home, and every day since that first day, Jack arrived promptly at nine.

Today nine came and went with no Jack. Selena glanced at her calendar and realized it was Sunday. Somehow, she had lost track of the days. She imagined Jack would spend the day with Theo. Selena looked out the window of her office, not really seeing the beautiful trees beyond. Dropping her forehead against the glass, she closed her eyes. She was so tired; she wasn't sure if she could stay on her feet much longer. The nightmares were depriving her of sleep, and Sullivan's presence in her home deprived her of peace of mind. His presence was as disturbing, perhaps even more so, than the nightmares.

"You need to take a break." Carter poked his head through Selena's half-open office door. Most days she kept the door firmly closed. He figured she was working when she shut the door. He pictured her behind her desk, working efficiently and without pause. But right now she wasn't working. Standing by the window, her gaze distant, she looked lost. Other than the time she'd cried at the hospital, he had not seen her as anything but in full control. Once she set foot back in her own home, she had gone back to the ice queen he'd gotten used to at the office. Perversely, he preferred her when she was ignoring him.

Selena pushed away from the window but didn't turn to face him. "I'm supposed to be at Jack's helping to set up the nursery with Theo and Isabelle."

Carter saw how stiff her spine was, and how tense she seemed. The week had certainly been stressful. He had been fielding phone calls from reporters all week who wanted to interview Selena about the shooting. He had Detective Quinlan checking in once a day to see if he and Jack had made any progress. Carter knew the detective would be doing everything he could to see if there was anyone else behind the shooting, but so far, all three of them had come up empty. It could be that the man known as Mallory was the one behind it and that this was over. But something about the shooting sat uneasily in his gut, and he had a feeling Jack and Mac had the same feeling.

Carter knew the two of them needed to get out of the house. Carter was feeling cooped up, but mostly he was feeling frustrated. And it wasn't the case that had him frustrated; it was the woman across the room from him. Sometimes when he saw her, desire would slam into his gut. The woman was beautiful. He had never been attracted to delicate women before, but something about the buried hint of fragility in her attracted him in ways he hadn't been before. She would probably slap him, possibly even punch him, if he were to act on his growing desire to kiss her. And he knew, without a doubt, kissing was not where he wanted any advance he made to end. He couldn't stop wondering if she'd be cold in bed, or if he would discover a buried passion. It was also the hint of fire he saw in her eyes on occasion that made his body ache to get closer.

"Does anyone know you were supposed to go over there today?" He knew security was tight around her, and he had a feeling her schedule was one of her best-kept secrets.

Selena sighed and faced him. She couldn't hide the strain on her face, or the disappointment she had been feeling since she looked at her calendar and what she had planned for the day. "Wallace knew. He's the only one who has access to my itinerary."

"Go on up and change. Be ready in twenty. We need to get out and setting up a nursery is as good an excuse as any." Carter left the office and headed upstairs.

Selena gaped at his receding back. Everything inside her rejected following his orders. Then she smiled ruefully. She could either obey him or spend another day working, trying to work herself hard enough to sleep. She'd rather see her friends and perhaps relax enough to sleep later. She climbed the stairs behind Sullivan, heading straight to her room to change. She sent a text to Theo letting her know she and Sullivan would arrive in a little over an hour.

They met at the front door. Carter still had his left arm in a cast. "Do you know how to drive?"

Selena was startled by the question and almost snapped at him, then realized it probably was a reasonable question. "Yes, I know how to drive. We'll take the Mercedes. It's my favorite."

Carter set the alarm as he followed her to the oversized detached garage. "How many cars do you have?"

"Mmm. I have four. I have a four x four truck. That's Wallace's favorite. Of course, he has a Porsche he's in love with and uses the truck only in bad weather. I also have an

SUV that I drive in bad weather. I have a convertible I rarely drive but drive more now that Theo and Isabelle want me to pick them up in it. And then I have the Mercedes sedan."

Carter just shook his head and kept his comments about spoiled brats to himself. He'd put his foot in his mouth enough over his feelings about her excessive ways.

Surprisingly, Selena was a good driver. Carter watched the speedometer and saw she rarely went over the limit. She drove the car competently and obeyed all the traffic laws. The years he was in law enforcement taught him how to be an offensive driver, and even now he often was guilty of speeding and breaking a few traffic laws.

About an hour later, Selena pulled into the driveway of a small bungalow. "This isn't quite what I pictured your friend Jack living in."

Selena closed her car door and set the locks. "They bought this just last month. With the baby coming, they decided both of their apartments were too small. Isabelle is a fantastic interior designer. If she ever gets out of the charity business, she could open up her own business."

"What type of charity?" He followed behind Selena, scanning the neighborhood.

"The Heart's Way Foundation. John and Isabelle work for the owner. Jack does business with the foundation and donates money. Theo recently started donating some of her free time, not that she's had much lately, what with opening her law firm."

Carter pointed to the car already in the driveway. "Is this their car?"

"Yes." Selena took the steps to the porch and turned to see Sullivan scanning the neighborhood. It was odd seeing him perform the task Wallace had been doing for the last six years. Just watching him, his face so intense, made her heart rate increase.

Selena rang the bell but didn't wait for it to be answered. "We're here."

The two couples turned to greet them from where they were sitting in the living room. Isabelle came and hugged Selena. "I'm so glad you're okay. When we heard what had happened, we wanted to come see you. Jack said it wasn't a good idea."

"Jack, Sullivan, and Detective Quinlan aren't convinced the shooter acted on his own. While I was in the hospital, it was probably best to keep away. Sullivan made sure we weren't followed on our way here, and most people wouldn't know to look for me here."

Theo carefully eased herself to her feet. "We're glad you could come. We have some stencils to paint on, and we have the furniture to arrange. And the crib you bought was delivered. It's beautiful. Our son will sleep in style."

Selena couldn't help the huge grin. "Yes, he will. And I'm so glad you like it."

"We love it." Theo glanced behind Selena to where the man stood. "Hi again, and welcome. We're so glad you brought her over."

Selena gestured to the other couple. "And this is John and Isabelle."

Carter shook their hands and took a seat. He watched as the three women quickly left the room.

Jack picked the conversation up. "Theo was happy when Selena texted and said she could make it. They've all been poring over baby decorating books for weeks. I don't care what the nursery looks like, just as long as it gets finished. The baby is due in three weeks."

John leaned back on the couch. "So how are you faring living with Selena? I hear you got the task of playing bodyguard while Ellis is laid up."

Carter relaxed on the overstuffed chair. "It's been all right. She barely leaves her home office. It's easy to guard someone behind prison walls."

Jack contemplated that. "Prison walls is a good analogy. She had the security fence, gate, and cameras installed before she even moved in. Not that I blame her."

"I imagine that with the type of business she's in, she could be a good target for robbery or kidnapping." Carter accepted the beer John handed him.

"Look, Jack and I thought it best to give you a heads-up on Selena. She'd be ticked if she knew we told you, so keep it to yourself. Selena's father is in prison for trying to murder her. Jack kept it out of the press when it happened, along with the trial. I only know because she told me when she became involved in the foundation. Didn't want it to be a surprise if I found out. Since then, she's had Ellis as a bodyguard. Within the first year of running the company on her own, she tripled the profits and bought her house outside the city."

Carter glanced to the hallway where he could hear the women's voices. His voice was cold when he spoke. "How close did he come?"

Jack saw where his gaze was. "Not as close as he'd have liked. He was trying to make it look like an accident. It didn't take long for her to realize her accidents weren't random instances. That's when she hired me. She's been paranoid ever since. And with the shooting, she's got to be feeling anxious."

Carter turned back to the two men. "You'd never know it. She's as cool as a cucumber."

Jack agreed. "It's one of her less charming qualities, but give her enough time, and she'll relax around you. And she's a great kisser."

John choked on his beer, then coughed. "I can't say I know that personally, but she does have a kissable mouth. Kissed her yet, Carter?"

Carter looked at the two men. It was obvious both of them had caught him staring at her. "No. And she's not my type."

"What's not your type? Beautiful? Rich? Smart?" Jack grinned and opened another beer.

"Cold. And probably the rich part." Carter took another swallow of his beer.

"You'd probably have to defrost her first. Can't do much about the money, but I wouldn't worry about it too much. She doesn't measure people by what they have. Trust me." John took out his wallet and pulled out a business card.

Carter took the card John held out to him. "What's this?"

John motioned to the card. "My business card. If you hang around Selena long enough, I'll eventually get you recruited to the foundation. You'll need to buy a tux. Selena is speaking at our charity event in a couple of weeks.

She'll be safe there. We've got top-of-the-line security, thanks to Jack."

Carter took a large swallow of his beer. "I don't think I've ever worn a tuxedo."

Jack smiled. "I'll email you the address of a shop that can get you outfitted. Just expense it to Powell Trading."

Carter relaxed once again when the men turned their attention to the game on television. He had a new perspective on Selena. Having your father try to murder you would probably make anyone paranoid. And given the nature of her business, she probably felt the need to have twenty-four-hour security.   But the foundation was probably the biggest revelation. Even though he knew most rich people donated money, he doubted many of them made personal appearances at charity functions where they were a key speaker. But really, a tux?

* * *

Selena helped Isabelle scoot the large crib to the corner of the room. The stencils had gone on easily enough, once Isabelle showed her how to do it. On her own, she probably would have made a mess. The end result was a blue, white, and gray boy's room that was beautiful and anything but ordinary. A new light fixture hung from the ceiling, Isabelle bought a mobile for the crib, and the dresser and changing table were now set up on the other side of the room.

An antique rocking chair had also been a gift from Selena when Jack told her he was expecting a baby. The rocking chair finished off the room. It had belonged to Selena's grandmother on her father's side. Jack had refused to take it at first because he knew it was a family heirloom, but he had accepted it when Selena insisted. Selena couldn't bring herself to have it on display in her home because it was a painful reminder of her father and his side of the family who now rejected her. They hadn't believed her accusations against him. Despite the family drama, she hadn't been able to get rid of it either. Giving it to Jack allowed the beautiful antique to find a new home.

Theo sat in the rocker and slightly rocked back and forth. Isabelle had gotten new cushions for it to match the room. "So how are you, really? It's got to be hard with Ellis in the hospital and a stranger in your home."

Selena took a seat on the floor, where Isabelle had already made herself comfortable. "He's not a stranger. He's been working for me for a couple of months. And he's a friend of Daniel's. But it hasn't been easy. I can't help but feel guilty about what happened to Wallace. He could have been killed."

Isabelle patted her knee. "I know it sounds harsh, but that's what you pay him for. That's what bodyguards do. But we're all glad Ellis will make a full recovery. Theo and I brought him cookies yesterday. He's got half the female hospital staff falling at his feet."

Selena leaned back on her hands. "That's Wallace. He's quite the charmer."

"What we can't figure out is why you two never got together. You practically live together, and he's really hot." Theo rubbed her belly while she continued rocking.

Selena gave an awkward shrug from where she sat. "He

went to work for me while I was still technically married, and it never went beyond work. He has a job to do, and despite his being 'hot,' we aren't attracted to each other."

"But you were to Jack." Theo didn't sound jealous. She already knew nothing had happened between the petite woman on her floor and her husband. But Selena's and her husband's friendship was a strong one.

"Same problem. I was married. Plus, though I enjoyed the time we spent together, we just didn't click." Selena left out the part where she'd kissed him a few times and how much she'd enjoyed it. She thought Jack probably had told her, but Selena wasn't going to go into details.

"So, what about Carter?" It hadn't gotten past Isabelle's attention the way Selena had glanced back to watch the man.

Selena relented and told the truth. She didn't think she could hide it if she wanted to. "The man's ridiculously attractive, and when I'm around him, he makes me ache."

Theo sighed. "Yeah, Jack makes me ache."

Isabelle lay down on her back, staring up at the ceiling. "Same here. I was half in love with John when I'd only seen his picture. When I met him, I realized how much I wanted to keep him. What are you going to do?"

Selena glanced at her friends. "What's there to do? He thinks I'm cold, selfish, materialistic, and spoiled."

Theo laughed. "I thought the same things until I got to know you. Let him get to know you. You keep people away. If you want to see if Carter can stop the ache, you'll have to let him get close to you, see who you truly are."

"Agreed." Isabelle sat back up. "We know you. We know how much you care about other people. Let Carter see the softer side of you."

Selena got to her feet. "There is no softer side. That part died a long time ago. And how do you know that what you see isn't the real me, anyway?"

Isabelle took her hand and pulled her back to the floor. "We just mean there's more than one side to you. There's the business side that has to be tough and savvy. But there's the part of you that buys baby cribs, helps decorate a nursery, and donates her time and money to helping others make the world a better place. You have a strong sense of right and wrong, and despite the wealth and the stuff you hide behind, you're there for your friends. And look at what you did for Daniel. You hired Carter because you felt sorry for your nephew and wanted to help him out. You might not have as soft a side as you did when you were younger, but it's still there, just a little bruised."

Selena would have argued further but couldn't. What she wanted to do was cry. These two women, people who had known her for less than a year, knew her better than anyone else. "Sullivan will be around for a while, so I guess we'll see what happens. Wallace put him in charge of my safety. I don't think Wallace will be back to work for a couple of months, so Sullivan is stuck with the job unless he quits."

Theo stopped rocking. "Not likely. He watches you. And if Ellis picked him, he believes he's the type of man to stick it out."

Selena knew that sticking it out was exactly what Sullivan would do. She supposed her problem was that she wanted him to see her as a woman, and a desirable one at that. She supposed she could try spending time with him, getting to know him better. Her friends were right about one thing. If she got used to him, she'd be more comfortable around him. She just didn't know if he would let her get close.

Chapter Six

Selena didn't get much chance to be alone with Sullivan. They got home late Sunday night. He seemed to enjoy the company of her friends, and for that, she was grateful. He went straight to bed when they got back. Selena had lain in bed, tossing and turning most of the night. Monday morning, Jack was back, and the two men went back to going through their lists. Jack wanted to get as much accomplished before he turned the case over to one of his colleagues. The baby could come any day, and once the baby was here, Jack was taking a short leave from work.

Tuesday and Wednesday were pretty much the same. Jack and Sullivan sat in her media room, listening to sports on the television while they sorted through the names. One thing that stood out was there had not been a single email threat since the shooting. It was beginning to look like Mallory might have been acting alone after all. Selena supposed it was time to get back to her normal routine. The press had already moved on, so it wasn't likely they would bother her at the office. And according to McCray, they had pretty much stopped calling.

Selena shut her computer down a little after five. She'd already been working since a little after six that morning. She was expecting a call from Wallace at any time. He had called her that morning to tell her the doctor was going to sign his release forms. The home health worker was already at Wallace's, waiting for his return. And given the amount of money Selena was paying the woman, she expected top-of-the-line service.

Selena stretched and rose from her desk. When she opened the door, she thought she heard music coming from the next room. The music drew her to the room as nothing else could have. She opened the door, her eyes fixed on the man behind the piano.

"Do you play?" Carter looked up and saw Selena standing in the doorway. He played a few more chords on the piano while he waited for an answer.

"No." Selena rested her hip against the doorframe when Sullivan looked up in disbelief.

"Then why do you own an incredibly expensive baby grand piano, along with all of these other instruments?"

Unable to resist provoking him, Selena cocked a brow at him and spoke without thinking about how she wanted to charm him, not put him off. "That's what rich people do. They buy things they'll never use. It's a music room, so I have musical instruments in it. I have a library here, too, so it's full of books I've never read and probably never will read. It goes along with the three cars I don't drive to fill the garage, and the swimming pool with a waterfall and hot tub in the large glass building behind the house that I pay to maintain but hardly use."

"It's a waste." Carter closed the lid on the keys. He had seen the large glass building but thought it was a greenhouse. But he supposed a large pool house was more her style. He looked back over at her. She was at home and wore an expensive suit and heels. Her face was made up, and she looked calm and put together. He hadn't even bothered to shave since he wasn't planning on going anywhere but to the hospital.

"I suppose it's a matter of perspective. The closet full of clothes I've only worn once could be considered a waste. I consider it part and parcel of who I am."

"Do you even know who you are? You're constantly surrounded by people telling you what to do and what to think. I'd say you have this house and all the stuff in it because you don't know who you are, and you think all this stuff will define you."

Selena gave him a small, tight smile. "You may have a point. Or maybe you're just like everyone else who can't see beyond the image in front of them. Or maybe it's that you see what you want to see. Reality doesn't matter; only perception."

Carter spun on the piano bench and straddled it. He ignored her comments. "What will you do when you run out of stuff to buy?"

"Some people would say you can never have enough stuff. But to answer your question, once I started to run out of stuff to buy, I started giving money away. Right now I'm doing that by employing my nephew's friend because my nephew made me feel sorry for him. And then that friend ended up in my home, criticizing me for my lifestyle while he makes himself comfortable, relaxing in my media room, eating a three-hundred-dollar jar of imported caviar, and putting his greasy fingers all over what is an incredibly expensive antique."

Carter watched her as she left him. He supposed he deserved that. But really, three-hundred-dollar caviar? The woman had no grasp of reality or what normal people went through. Her entire home was filled with expensive things, but from what he could tell from his short time there, she found no enjoyment in the things she surrounded herself with. She had a music room she didn't use, a library for show, a media room that looked like she rarely set foot in it, and a huge piece of land she didn't spend any time tending.

He followed her out into the hall and watched her as she went to the door that led to her home office. He realized for the first time that she was practically a prisoner here. He remembered saying it before to Jack and John, but he hadn't realized how true his words were. Her prison was beautiful and opulent, but a prison, nonetheless. She paid for her jailer in the form of Ellis. He was always nearby, ready to secret her away at a moment's notice. She was never alone, never allowed herself privacy outside of her bedroom and office. He didn't know how she didn't go crazy. Her constant isolation was starting to bother him because he didn't see a need for it. Yes, she owned an antiquities business, and billions of dollars of goods flowed through the doors of her business, but he didn't understand the self-imposed prison. And it had started long before the shooting. Going to her friend's house was the only time she'd expressed a need to get out and breathe.

Angered by both himself and her, he followed her to her office. He didn't bother knocking; instead, he opened the door. "I've had enough. When Ellis was shot, you were all soft and feminine. You showed real emotions, or what I thought were real emotions. You set foot back in your house, and you put a wall between you and anyone or anything that would upset the isolation you've made for yourself. Which is real?"

Selena stood by the window, frozen in place at the anger she saw on his face. Instead of confronting him, she turned her back. It was a mistake.

Carter quickly crossed the room and spun Selena to face him. He backed her into the corner. He could see anger flags high on her cheeks, and her chest was heaving with the force of her breathing. "Don't turn away from me."

"Get your hands off me." Selena tried to draw back, but he had gotten so close to her. The wall prevented her from moving.

Carter realized his hands were gripping her shoulders. He loosened his grip but didn't let her go. "I want to know. Which is the real you?"

Selena gazed up into his eyes. The deep brown depths held a real curiosity. Instead of wanting to pull away, she desperately wanted to press herself closer. Only the knowledge that he would most likely reject her if she did kept her in place. Then she registered the question, and her anger fled. A deep numbness settled in its place. "There is a saying that goes something to the effect that it's not who you are in public that is the real you; it's who you are when no one is watching. In my home, where I'm alone, it's as real as it gets. What you see is what you get."

Carter brushed Selena's hair back with the tips of his fingers. His mouth was only inches from hers. "Sometimes I believe that. Then other times, I don't. I saw how relaxed you were with your friends. And when you came out of the nursery, with paint on your fingers, you were truly happy. Then you come home, and you freeze up. You barely speak to me. Even Jack, whom you have a thing for, gets subjected to the cold treatment."

"I don't have a 'thing' for Jack." Selena wet her lips, her gaze still focused on Sullivan's eyes.

"No? You couldn't prove it by me. Then again, I did see you kiss Ellis. But then again, Jack tells me you're a great kisser."

That startled her. "Really? I would say the same about him."

For some reason, her casual admittance of the former relationship, even if it was just a few kisses, irritated him. Standing this close to her, smelling the sweet scent of her skin, he wanted a taste. He was probably risking his job, but Carter leaned closer until their mouths were just a breath apart.

Selena closed her eyes, wanting and accepting what she knew would be a kiss that would permanently change their relationship. She lifted a hand to Sullivan's shoulder, rising on her toes.

Her office line interrupted the pair.

Selena jerked her head away, and her sudden movement had Sullivan stepping back. She quickly went to pick up the phone.

Carter took a deep breath, unsure of what had just happened between them. Once his head cleared, he realized Selena was talking to Ellis.

"We can be there in an hour. Yes. Okay. Bye." Selena

set the phone back in its cradle.

"I take it the doctor released him." Carter took another deep breath and a couple of steps back.

Selena took a couple of calming breaths before grabbing her purse. "I'll drive again. You should keep that arm relaxed."

Carter followed behind her, oddly touched by her offhand comment about his arm. The thing hurt pretty bad, not that he'd admit it to her; and being his dominant arm, he was content to let her drive. He also needed to keep an eye out for anyone following them on the road. He could do that more easily with her driving. It also helped keep the gun that hung discreetly under his jacket easily accessible.

The ride to the hospital was uneventful. The pair was silent as they made their way to Ellis's room.

Ellis glanced up, relief on his face. "Get me the heck out of here."

Selena smiled at him. "You are always grumpy when you don't feel well."

Ellis stood, nodding to his bag for Carter to take. "The nurse said she would get a wheelchair to take me to the car."

Selena left the room to find the nurse. Carter watched her treating form.

"Find anything yet?" Ellis waited until Selena was out of earshot.

Carter nodded. "Jack and I think we have a lead on a man named Cameron Matthews. Seems a large cash payment came out of his account and into the account of Mallory, the guy who shot you. So far, we've been unable to identify this Matthews character. We're pretty sure it's an alias. Whoever created it did a good job. Matthews's identity is well hidden. It will take time to trace him. I think when we find him, we'll find who was behind the shooting. Question is motive."

Ellis took that in. "Selena was the target, no doubt. But you're right. Why? Other than her job, she keeps a low profile."

"In her personal life, yes. But she's a well-known public figure. And from what I've been able to ascertain, she sticks her nose into a lot of other people's business. And many of those people wouldn't appreciate it if they knew she was the one who turned them in to the authorities."

Ellis looked closely at the man standing across the room. There was more to Carter than met the eye. "Good job. Not too many people would have been able to track Selena's activities."

Carter acknowledged the compliment. "Not too many people in Selena's shoes would care. One thing I've learned is that she has a strong sense of right and wrong. And she does what she can to balance the scales. It's very admirable."

"There's a lot about her to admire. But I can see you don't need to be told that. But that's professionally. Personally, there's more to her than meets the eye."

"That I'm not so sure of. But I think you and Jack are biased." Carter looked out the door to see Selena talking to someone at the front desk.

Ellis cocked a brow. "Really? You may be right. She and Jack are close, which is why I'm glad you're helping with the investigation. He's too close. It's my job to stick by her side. But given that you're the one who noticed the gun, I'd say perhaps I was too close, too. I'd become complacent where her safety is concerned."

Carter looked back at Ellis. "You can't blame yourself for what happened. That was one well-planned execution. If you hadn't reacted as quickly as you did, your boss would be dead."

Ellis nodded but kept silent. It certainly was a well-planned execution. But it was his job to anticipate and prevent. He'd failed. That knowledge was an acid sitting deep in his gut.

Selena came back into the room, along with transport. Selena saw Wallace wince as he settled into the wheelchair, and it alarmed her that he was even willing to allow himself to be wheeled out. But she had no doubt he'd recuperate better in his own home. "There is a home health worker at your house. She came highly recommended. She'll take care of you; make sure you're fed."

Ellis looked over at Selena. "Home health worker? Is she cute?"

Selena laughed. "Nope. But she's very capable, which is better."

Ellis leaned back in the wheelchair and relaxed until they arrived at the entryway. The Mercedes was waiting. Carter helped him into the passenger seat and took the seat in the back. Selena drove them back to the estate and parked in front of his home.

A very large, very strong-looking woman exited his front door. Ellis got a good look. He glanced at Selena suspiciously. "You did that on purpose."

She smiled serenely at him. "Yep. If I had hired some

cute, young woman, you'd have had her wrapped around your finger in no time. I need someone here who can boss you around and make sure you get better. And there will be a physical therapist coming in to help you with getting your strength back."

Between Carter and the nurse, a robust woman named Roxanne, Ellis was settled into his bed. Selena tugged the covers up over his chest and placed a kiss on his cheek. "You need to get some rest. If you need anything, have Roxanne ring the house. I'll see to it that you get it."

Ellis took Selena's hand, caressing her delicate fingers with his much larger, blunter ones. "I want you to promise me you won't do anything rash or stupid. Stay with Carter. Don't leave the house again until we catch the man responsible for the attack."

Selena glanced up at Sullivan. Her eyes narrowed. It became obvious he knew something she didn't. Instead of confronting him, she turned her gaze back to Wallace. "I promise. And I also promise Daniel will be heading your way. He said he wants to hold his monthly poker game at your house tomorrow night."

Ellis smiled. "That'd be nice. Maybe he can sneak me a beer."

Selena brushed the hair back from his forehead. "I've no doubt he could sneak one in. But just one until you're on your feet."

Carter took Selena's hand and led her outdoors. "He'll be fine."

"You should pop in tomorrow night for the game; make sure he doesn't overdo it." Selena climbed into the driver's seat and drove to the main house.

Carter came around and opened her door.

Selena opened the front door and turned off the alarm. "So, are you going to tell me what has Wallace so uptight about my security?"

Carter watched as Selena walked to her office and poured herself a drink. He had no choice but to follow her. She looked mad.

"Well?" Selena tossed back the drink and poured herself another.

"Jack and I found a bank account and a large transfer of cash. But we haven't found the man behind the alias."

Selena tossed back the second drink. "Alias? I trusted you and Jack to keep me apprised of your progress. Apparently, that isn't the case."

Carter took the bottle and the glass from her before she poured a third. "Jack and I don't have anything concrete. We have an alias but not the real person."

"But you have proof that Mallory was hired. Don't you think that's something I should know?"

"It won't help you sleep better at night." Carter poured himself a drink but only sipped it.

"What does my sleeping have to do with it?" Selena went to the sideboard and poured a sparkling water. The alcohol was going straight to her head on her empty stomach.

"Don't think I can't tell. You have dark circles under your eyes. You hide them well, but they are there. I hear you in the middle of the night, pacing your room. You're having nightmares, and knowing someone paid to have you murdered isn't going to ease them."

The room spun a little when Selena turned back to face him. "If you know I'm up at night, then you're not getting any more sleep than I am. And I am not paying you to worry about my lack of sleep. I'm paying you to find a killer. If you have a name, I can trace it."

Carter wanted to go to her. She was trembling, and it wasn't because of the alcohol. He poured her a third drink and handed it to her. "I can't promise that drinking yourself into oblivion will make you feel better, but it might help you sleep tonight."

Selena took the drink from his hand but just held it. He was right about one thing: having it confirmed that someone else was out there who wanted her dead was not going to help her sleep. "The alias's name?"

Carter led her to the sofa, pushing her lightly onto it. He took a seat next to her. "Cameron Matthews. The man doesn't exist anywhere but on paper. Jack is running his name through every system he has access to. No hits yet."

"Jack won't be working past this week. Theo is expecting any day now. I'll start running the name. I've got access to the same databases from my laptop." Selena tipped her head back against the sofa.

"I would start with the men you've sent to jail." Carter took the drink from her hand.

Selena glanced up at him, a startled look on her face. "And what do you know of it?"

Carter smiled. "I've got my sources. And I've been digging around your computer files. It wasn't hard to figure out. You've been responsible for at least six men going to prison in the past five years. Given the complexity of the scams they were running, that's quite impressive. You have some of the best computer security available, but no system is infallible. It's possible someone was able to trace the evidence from the authorities back to you."

Selena thought it highly unlikely. "I've got several safeguards in place. And should anyone have come close to tracing those files back to me, an alert would have triggered in my system. It is not impossible, but highly improbable that I was back hacked."

"When Ellis is feeling better, I will have him take a deep dive into the system. I agree it's unlikely, but not impossible. Your everyday clients are not going to want you harmed. But you've refused to do business with some powerful men. One of them might want revenge."

Selena rose on wobbly legs. "That's probably a more likely scenario. I'll get started on it tomorrow. I'm going to bed."

Carter looked at the clock on the far wall. It was later than he realized. "I'll follow you up."

Selena took the stairs quickly. "And Sullivan?"

"Yeah?" He looked up at her, her body slim and trembling.

"No more secrets. Despite what Wallace said, I will fire you. You tell me what you and Jack find when you find it, or you won't be here."

Carter just shrugged. "I'd like to see you try."

Selena gaped, no words coming to mind. "Good night, Sullivan."

"Good night, Selena."

* * *

Selena spent the day in her home office running the name Cameron Matthews through her computer. She let Jack and Sullivan continue their investigation from her media room. This would be Jack's last day working on the investigation, at least from her house. Theo had been complaining of back pain, and she was showing early signs of labor. Theo's doctor was convinced it would only be a day or two before they became parents.

As for Wallace, she'd been getting regular status reports from Roxanne. He had slept through the night and had already slept most of the day. Daniel was due in the next hour or so, and she thought he might be what Wallace needed to cheer him up. The doctor had warned her he might experience some depression or anxiety after the shooting. It was hard to picture Wallace, who had been her pillar of strength for so long, being anything but confident. But something wasn't right in the way he was behaving, and she knew guilt was eating at him. She wished there were something she could do but figured a guys' night would probably go a lot further toward lifting his spirits than anything she could do.

"Any luck?" Jack poked his head through her office door.

"No more than you two had. Whoever he is, he has hidden his tracks well. I found a couple more offshore bank accounts that might be tied to the same man, but I've been unable to find any other names. I did find the name of a business though. I tracked some money to NSWE Trading."

"What?" Jack came around. NSWE Trading was the

name of a trading company that had been owned by Colm O'Carroll, the drug-smuggling hitman who had tried to murder his wife. But the man was dead, and the company defunct. It didn't make sense.

"That was my first reaction. It doesn't make sense. Colm is dead, and the company doesn't exist. Someone resurrected the business, or at least the name, to hide funds."

"It doesn't add up. Someone would have to know you were involved in the investigation last year. And even if they did, what's in it for them? The Feds got involved and rounded up both the drug and the antiquities smugglers. And you didn't have a hand in that."

"No, but I did have a hand in finding Colm. But, as I said, he's dead. Who would have an interest in him? Both of the Marinos are in jail."

Jack leaned out the doorway and yelled for Carter. "I've got to go. Selena found something interesting. I'm going to dig from home, but get her to tell you the story. I want to know if there is anyone out there tied to Colm O'Carroll."

Selena didn't have to ask why. Jack was worried about a potential threat to Theo. "Call if you find anything. And have Isabelle call me when Theo goes into labor."

Carter saw Jack out. Daniel's poker game was going to start in about half an hour. "What was that all about? Who is Colm O'Carroll?"

Selena took a seat. "Long story short, he tried to kill Theo."

That took Carter by surprise. "Perhaps you should start at the beginning."

"You wouldn't have been working as a cop then, but do

you remember the murder of a man named Brandon Donovan?"

"He was the CEO of a law firm. He was murdered by his boss. A hit, from what I remember. Something to do with his son and drug smuggling."

"That's right. Angelo Marino was a partner in a law firm owned by him, his brother, and his cousin. His son, Angelo Jr., had gotten into drugs. Turns out he was working for Donovan, who was secretly blackmailing his boss. Angelo hired Colm O'Carroll to murder Donovan. O'Carroll was a competitor of mine."

Carter wasn't putting the pieces together. "What does this have to do with Theo?"

"Theo was the one who found Donovan's body. Her father, Thomas Landry, who owns the firm where Jack is now half-owner, is Theo's father. He was worried Theo might be a target. Theo was the one person, besides those involved, who knew Donovan had been smuggling drugs. Theo worked for Angelo Marino, and when she tried to take evidence to him that Donovan was not who he seemed, he fired her. Jack was tasked with protecting her. Landry had Jack dig into Donovan's activities when Theo had been fired. Found out that Donovan was definitely up to his ears with a drug cartel. But they are not the ones who killed him. Angelo Senior ordered the hit. O'Carroll was involved in dealing drugs and antiquities through his business. One of his antiquities clients was Angelo Senior. I knew that because Angelo had come to me, trying to get me to make some deals on his behalf. I refused."

"How were you involved?" Carter was learning how

Selena operated. She would have gotten involved in the investigation against a fellow antiquities dealer making illegal deals.

"Jack started putting feelers out. I picked up the thread. Did some digging. Wallace, too. O'Carroll was bad news. He inherited several companies when his father died. Before his father's death, he had been using the business to smuggle drugs. Then he realized smuggling antiquities made more money. Except he got caught, and his dad bailed him out. Later it came out that he had murdered his father. He was an addict, and he was also friends with Angelo Marino, Jr., who was also an addict. The two of them had a nice business going. Donovan used the knowledge of what O'Carroll and Junior were up to to blackmail Senior. He didn't take it too kindly, and Senior had Donovan murdered. He hired O'Carroll to do it."

"How convenient. Again, how were you involved?" Carter asked her.

"I told Jack about O'Carroll, and how he was tied to Marino Sr. Jack was trying to figure out who killed Donovan. Donovan was interested in politics, and Jack thought that might be the link. Turned out one of Donovan's donors was O'Carroll's father. From there I helped piece it together. I tracked cash payments from Senior to O'Carroll. Jack eventually got enough evidence, with the help of Detective Macaulay Quinlan, to arrest Senior. Junior and O'Carroll went underground. I had a trace on Theo's and Jack's activities and found out one of them hacked into Theo's flight plans. Jack and Landry called Detective Quinlan. Between the three of them, they captured Junior, and Colm was killed when he attempted to fire at Theo."

Carter thought about what she said, but there was still a piece missing. "With O'Carroll dead, the business went under. What does that have to do with Mallory?"

"I've been running Cameron Matthews through the database. I found some potential bank accounts offshore. And I found a payment from Matthews to NSWE Trading, the company O'Carroll owned. It went under completely when the Feds raided it. Several members of a South American drug cartel were arrested, as well as a couple of local government officials."

Carter swore. "And you were tied to the case?"

Selena shook her head. "No, that's why it's odd. After I did preliminary searches on O'Carroll, Jack called me off. Other than tracking him and Theo, I did pull out. Nothing in the investigation can be tied to either me or Jack. And Theo's name was never released, so no one knows she was involved. That's why Jack's worried. Nothing should tie any of us to NSWE or to any investigation into the drug cartel."

Carter rubbed his brow. "So why would money paid out to Mallory also have been paid out to a now non-existent antiquities company?"

Selena didn't have an answer. All she had were more questions. "I'll keep the search up. See what else I can find. You should go."

Carter crossed the room to where Selena stood. "Has anyone ever told you that you're a dangerous woman?"

Selena thought of Jack. "As a matter of fact, yes. But I

wouldn't worry about it too much. We're on the same side."

Carter cupped Selena's chin with his hand. No woman so delicate-looking should be so smart. It was a dangerous combination. And it turned him on. Instead of kissing her as he so wanted to, he released her chin and left the room.

Selena stood still, watching Sullivan until he was out of sight. Trembling, she braced herself against her desk. For a moment, she had seen raw desire in his eyes. Men desired her. Her husband had. Jack had. There had been a few other men over the years that had. But no man, not even Jack, made her tremble the way Sullivan did. If she didn't get a grip, she would be begging him to make love to her. She had a feeling he wouldn't turn her down, but she wanted more from him than sex. She wanted him to desire her, the real Selena, not the outer woman she presented to the world. But as he had said, did she even know who she was? She wasn't sure she knew the answer to that question anymore.

Chapter Seven

"Three kings." Ellis tossed his cards down.

Daniel groaned and tossed his cards down without showing them. "Figures."

Carter took a swallow of his beer and tossed his cards. "You got me."

Ellis grinned. "Like taking candy from a baby."

Daniel smiled and handed Ellis another beer. "Here, have another. I need to win my money back. I've got a business to run, you know."

"Is this why you couldn't afford to pay me?" Carter teased him, taking a long pull on his beer. He'd already lost a hundred bucks, but he was a little too buzzed from the few beers he had drunk to care. Not to mention, his current boss was paying him a ridiculous amount of money; the lost hundred wouldn't be noticed.

Ellis took the beer but didn't open it. "A little liquor won't ruin my winning streak."

Daniel, who had already drunk more than his usual amount, found that hilarious.

Carter, feeling parental, scooted Daniel's beer out of his reach. "Take it easy. At the rate you're going, you'll be passed out and unable to win back your money."

Daniel placed an arm around Carter's shoulders. "Isn't he great?"

Since Daniel wasn't asking anyone in particular, both men just nodded. They played a few more hands before Daniel excused himself. A few minutes later, he was snoring on Ellis's sofa.

"Got to hand it to him, he plays well for a kid. Needs to learn to hold his beer better." Ellis shuffled and dealt another hand.

Carter finished his beer and picked up his cards. "He grows on you; I'll say that for him."

"Selena loves that kid. You'd never know he was related to Selena's sister. That woman is cold."

"And Selena's not?" Carter tossed a couple of cards and picked up new ones.

"I like to think of her as reserved. If you took a good look, you'd see for yourself."

Carter snorted at that, then had to right himself when he felt a little dizzy. "She's hot. I'll give her that. That slim, curvy body makes a man's hands itch."

"That it does." Ellis tossed one card onto the pile.

Carter's eyes narrowed. "Excuse me?"

Ellis couldn't help feeling smug. "Man, you've got it bad."

"And you don't?" Carter lost interest in the cards.

"When I first met her, I thought like you did. Thought she was cold, distant. And in some ways, she is those things. But she has her reasons. And I can't say I blame her."

Carter thought back to the conversation he had with Jack and John. "John said her father tried to kill her."

Ellis's brows rose at the admission, but he didn't refute it. "Yes, he did. He staged a few 'accidents' and she got suspicious. Besides Daniel, her father was the only real family she had. Finding out he tried to kill her broke something inside her. Selena was already estranged from her brother and sister because she chose to inherit their mother's shares in her father's business instead of selling out. They believed she turned her back on them in favor of her father. It was a smart business move, but that isn't why she did it. Her father was destroying the business. The company had belonged to her grandfather. She couldn't bear to see it go under."

"How did you get involved with her? I know Jack investigated her father and helped convict him."

Ellis thought about how much to tell him. Some things were for Selena, and only Selena, to share. "Once she got over the initial shock, she realized she would have known what her father was doing had she been able to access his computer records. Jack explained to her how he had found the evidence against him. Once the trial was over, and her father was in prison, she wanted not only twenty-four-hour security but also someone who could teach her how to use a computer as a weapon. Jack recommended me. She liked what she saw and hired me. She then bought her house and installed every security measure available. And at the time, money was tight at the company, but she pulled the cash together."

"So why didn't you act on your itch?" Carter couldn't imagine any man living with Selena for any length of time and not wanting to find his way into her bed.

Ellis leaned back. "You'd have to have known her six years ago. She was so vulnerable, though she hid it well. It would have been cruel to take advantage of her, and she was interested in Jack. But she wasn't ready for any kind of relationship. It's one of the reasons she and Jack never went anywhere. We sort of drifted into this odd mentor/mentee relationship. And at some point, we became friends. Sex ruins friendships, plus she never gave me a single hint that she was interested. Now, you, she's interested in."

Carter thought about how she had brought her mouth closer to his when he would have kissed her. He remembered how she had trembled just a few hours before when he'd cupped her chin. It was still hard for him to reconcile her physical reactions to him with the cold woman he normally saw. "What makes you think she'd give me the time of day?"

Ellis got to his feet, swaying a bit. He knew Roxanne was in the next room waiting for him to fall on his face. She had warned him against drinking. He figured he'd better call it a night before he did. "Just trust me. She watches you. Has since the day she met you. All you have to do is make your move, and she'd be putty in your hands."

"She keeps her distance from me. I don't see desire when I look at her. I see something between disdain and disinterest."

Ellis nodded. "I know that look. She's good at keeping men at a distance. It's why she uses men's last names instead of their first. It helps keep her relationships with men impersonal. Daniel and Jack are the only exceptions. I've been Wallace since she met me. At work, it's McCray, not Martin. I suppose John is an exception, too, but that's because he's married to her friend. It's the same with all of her male clients and acquaintances. But trust me, give her a chance. She deserves to be happy, and I have a feeling you'd make her very happy."

Carter wondered why all the men in Selena's life were trying to force the two of them together. Jack had told him what a great kisser she was and told him to find out for himself. Ellis told him to make a move on her, and, man, was it tempting. As drunk as he was, it sounded like an excellent idea.

Ellis let Roxanne take him to bed, and Carter did a quick check on Daniel. He was still snoring away on the sofa.

Carter made his way across the lawn, the bright lights from the security system illuminating the path. He opened the door, punched in the security code, and then reset it.

"I wasn't expecting you back tonight. Did you have fun?" Selena was at the top of the stairs, dressed in her nightgown, with a thin robe covering it. She had left her bed when she heard the alarm being disarmed.

Carter was sure he could see the outline of her body through the thin material. The top of her lush breasts was revealed by the low cut. He took the stairs two at a time. He wanted a taste.

Selena took a step back when Sullivan would have run into her. She could smell beer on his breath. Feeling indulgent, she took his arm and led him to his bedroom.

In a smooth move, Carter brought Selena up against him, pressing her body against his bedroom door. He buried his lips against her throat. "Has anyone ever told you how beautiful you are?"

Selena shivered when Sullivan's mouth moved from her neck to the top of her breasts. She realized her robe was open. She lifted her hand to close it, but Sullivan's mouth moved from one breast to the other, and her hand fell away. His hands were caressing her hips, his fingers finding their way around to her backside. She felt the bold caress, her nightgown and robe offering her no protection from his touch. All she wanted was to melt against him.

"You make me ache." Carter's hands molded her bottom, his body pressing against hers. The scent of her that lingered between her breasts had his mouth nuzzling the fabric aside. He found a nipple with his tongue, and it hardened under his mouth.

Selena's hands went to his hair. He held her so close to him that she could feel his erection pressed against her belly. She wanted to bring his mouth closer, to allow him full access to her breasts, but instead, she used her grip on his hair to pull him away. "Sullivan, you need to stop. You're drunk."

"Carter. My name is Carter. I want you to say it."

"Sullivan, let's get you to bed."

The beer that had only made him feel dizzy earlier was now making the room spin. Keeping his hands on Selena's bottom, he walked backward into the bedroom. He fell onto the bed, pulling Selena with him.

Selena felt one of his legs slide between hers. She wanted nothing more than to straddle his body and let him take her where he would. But he was drunk, and he would regret it in the morning, assuming he even remembered. She slithered off him, not an easy feat. His hands were attempting to remove her gown, but the robe was in the way. Had he been sober, his grip would have been too strong, and she wouldn't have been able to get away. Of course, if he were sober, she wouldn't have found herself in this situation in the first place.

Carter's eyes opened when she moved off the bed, the room now spinning around him. "I want to be inside you."

Selena closed her eyes, her body reacting to his very frank statement. Her body ached, just as he said his did. But he hadn't even kissed her. His bold movements were of a man who was interested in sex and nothing more. And though she had no doubt sex with Sullivan would be off the charts, she was beginning to have real feelings for him. Those feelings scared her. She was afraid that if she let him make love to her, she'd have no defenses left.

Leaving him where he lay, she returned to her bedroom. She felt hot tears sting her eyes. She pulled up her covers and simply lay on her side, staring at the wall. She could feel his mouth on her breasts, his hands caressing her. Oh, how she wanted to throw caution to the winds. She had imagined him doing any number of things to her body, making love to her in just about every room in her home. She thought she hid her desire well, but she was now afraid she wouldn't be able to anymore, now that she'd had a taste. And she feared that if she let him close, he would break her heart.

* * *

The night was a restless one. Selena tossed the covers off when she saw the clock turn six. At one in the morning, she had indulged in a hot soak, hoping to relax enough to sleep.

At some point, she fell asleep, only to awaken again when the early morning sunlight started to come through her curtains.

Selena brushed out her hair but didn't bother to get dressed. Pulling on a sturdier and less see-through robe, she tiptoed to Sullivan's bedroom door. She could hear the shower going. She turned back to the stairs and headed to the kitchen. She had a feeling they both were going to need extra caffeine today. And deciding that a little food wouldn't hurt either of them, she popped four slices of whole-grain bread in the toaster and pulled out a tub of butter and some jam.

Twenty minutes later, Carter found Selena in the kitchen. He had pulled on a fresh pair of jeans and a clean t-shirt. Since he looked as scruffy as he felt, he had run a razor over his face. Along with the morning had come his memory of the night before. He had practically assaulted Selena last night. He remembered backing her up against his bedroom door. He remembered helping himself to the lush treasures he'd seen exposed in the flowy nightgown. What he couldn't remember well was Selena's response to those advances.

Wary of what might greet him, he just offered her a brief good morning.

Selena turned to see him hovering in the doorway of the kitchen. "Come on in and grab a cup of coffee. I figured that after a night of drinking, you might like to have some toast with it."

Carter was still feeling a bit wary of her reactions to him, but she seemed almost friendly this morning. He took both the coffee she handed him and the plate of toast. He took a seat on the stool at the island where she was slathering strawberry jam on hers.

"How do you feel this morning?" Selena took a sip of her coffee while she studied Sullivan. He hadn't said anything other than good morning to her. He was drinking the coffee as if the caffeine in it were the only thing keeping him on his feet.

"I'm hungover. I can't remember the last time I drank that much. I didn't drink this much when I quit the force."

Selena took the opportunity to ask one of the many questions she had about him. "You never did say why you quit."

Sensing real interest in his answer, Carter thought for a moment about how much to tell her. It had been a very hard, very personal decision to quit. And it was hard to admit that part of it was fear. "No, I didn't. As you said, I didn't have to. But I hated sitting at a desk. And when I was let back out in the field, I'd lost my edge. I was no good to myself or my partner. The psychologist at the department felt that finding a different line of work was my best option. I took his advice and quit."

"It's hard to imagine you losing your edge. You stepped right into the line of fire when Wallace was shot. Maybe your edge was just dulled for a while. I imagine being shot was traumatic." Selena pushed the jam his way since he seemed to be staring at it instead of looking at her.

Carter hadn't thought about it one way or the other when shots were fired. She had a point, though. He hadn't run for cover when bullets started flying; he'd run toward them. Ellis had taken three body shots, and Selena was next. He'd taken the shot that killed Mallory, and he hadn't hesitated. His biggest fear had been that he would freeze in a situation involving gunfire. He'd feared for his life and that of those around him. He'd quit instead of finding out.

Both were quiet for a few minutes. But then Carter realized he owed her for that insight. "Thank you, Selena."

Her head jerked upward, confusion on her face. "For what?"

Carter gave her a crooked smile. "For taking your chances on a burnt-out ex-cop. That day in your office could have gone very differently had I froze."

She realized what he meant. "You were afraid that if you were put in the same situation that got you shot, you'd freeze up and get someone killed."

Carter was once again quiet but slightly nodded his head in agreement. He didn't want to talk about the day he was shot. When he'd stepped into the line of fire to protect Selena from a gunman, he hadn't given it any thought. And he hadn't given it a single thought afterward, either. It's just what he did. He owed her for showing him he hadn't been permanently damaged by the crazed man who had fired at him and his team.

Selena ate her toast and finished a second cup of coffee. Sullivan ate one of the two slices but was more interested in the coffee. She poured him a third cup. "I hope your hangover fades because I have a tailor coming in today. I forgot to tell you."

"A what?" Carter looked up at her. He'd been doctoring his coffee when she dropped that bombshell.

"We don't have time to get you a custom tux for Saturday, so I ordered you one. And I ordered you shoes and socks. The tailor is coming by to alter the tux to fit and is bringing a few pairs of shoes for you to try on. He's also dropping off the dress I bought last month. There's a charity event, and I have to attend."

Carter scowled. "You shouldn't be in public right now. Someone tried to kill you, if you'll recall."

"Yes, I know. But security at the event is tight. Wallace always attended with me. I'll need to introduce you to Kevin. He's my date." Selena picked up his plate and dumped his toast in the trash. She put the rest of the dishes, minus his coffee cup, in the dishwasher.

Carter scowled at the word date. He should have known she'd have one. How could he forget he was working for one of the most sought after women in the city? She'd dated politicians, businessmen, and a few lawyers if he recalled correctly. Every other month or so, she'd have a new man on her arm. The sudden surge of jealousy was unwelcome.

"And if I tell you that you can't go?" Sullivan stood, using his height to intimidate her.

"We both know you're getting paid to keep an eye on me. One call from McCray and I can have you replaced."

"You can fire me, Selena, but you can't get rid of me that easily. Whether you pay me or not, I'm not going anywhere until we find out who wants you dead."

Selena stared. "You're serious."

Carter picked up his coffee. "Very. Get used to it."

Selena watched him as he left the kitchen and headed to the media room. Feeling a bit off guard, she went back upstairs to shower and dress.

For most of the morning, they both worked from their normal locations. She had been more than slightly amused when the tailor had shown up and measured Sullivan for his tux. Then he'd grumbled about the shoes. Then he'd blown up when he had picked up the invoice showing how much his new outfit was going to cost. He'd spent a good fifteen minutes arguing about what else that money could buy, and that she had lost her mind if she thought some fabric was worth the cash she was spending. Unable to resist, she had patted his cheek. His eyes had darkened threateningly for a moment, but he'd quickly gotten himself under control.

Two hours later, the tailor finished up his sewing, and Sullivan was standing in her office decked out in his new tux. Selena was admiring the tailor's handiwork when her cell rang. She saw the number and stepped out into the hall.

"Hello, Kevin. I wasn't expecting to hear from you until Saturday." Selena turned her back when she saw Sullivan standing just outside her office so he could eavesdrop on the conversation.

"I just got back from Italy. I heard about what happened at your office. Are you okay?" Kevin's voice was slightly distracted as he asked.

"Yes. As I'm sure you heard, Wallace was seriously injured but survived the shooting. Why did you call?"

Kevin gave her an exasperated sigh. "I called to tell you I won't be picking you up on Saturday. I can't put myself in danger. Rumors are floating all over the place. You should have talked to the press. They were hounding my office while I was away."

Selena felt a surge of anger. "Of course, it wasn't my intention to inconvenience your staff. You have my assurance I won't be calling you."

"This isn't how I wanted this to end, but we both know it was inevitable."

Selena tried to rein in her temper. "Yes, we both knew. But I didn't think it would be because you're a coward."

"I can see you're not going to be rational about this. Good bye, Selena."

She hit the end button on her phone. She supposed she wasn't exactly upset with him, and she supposed she couldn't blame him either. But it certainly was a bit of a hit to her ego that he cared so little for her that he could blow her off when something so incredibly awful had happened.

"I take it that was your date for Saturday." Carter tugged at the collar of his new shirt.

"Yes, it was. And now he'll go back to his friends and tell them how I had become completely irrational and how he just had to break it off."

Carter raised his brow at that. "That happen a lot?"

"More often than you probably think. I date men with big egos and a major streak of selfishness. It usually works out for a while. Then when things don't go the way they planned, they break it off. They blame me for it, and I suppose they have the right of it. It's not hard to find some other woman willing to stroke their egos, along with other parts of their anatomy."

Carter felt another irrational surge of jealousy when he thought of Selena's soft hands on another man, no matter what part of their anatomy. "Maybe you should date a different kind of man."

Selena brushed past Sullivan and went back into her office. The tailor was waiting patiently for her to sign his invoice. She took the paper from him and signed it.

"I'll see myself out." The man discreetly left. The front door alarm told them he'd left.

"Well?" Sullivan leaned against the doorjamb.

"You should take off that tux. You're going to wrinkle it."

"For what you paid, it shouldn't wrinkle. And you're avoiding the question."

Selena thought to feign ignorance but decided it was a waste of time. "Yes, I should probably date a different type of man. But I date for business reasons, not personal ones. When I'm ready for a relationship that could end with a real commitment, I'll look at a different pool of men."

Carter crossed the room. He looked down into her eyes for a moment. Then he gently cupped her cheek in his palm. "And when do you think you might be ready to do that?"

Selena couldn't look away from him. She placed her hand over his. "I think I'm getting closer every day."

Carter brushed her other cheek with the back of his fingers. "Good. Don't make another date for Saturday."

Selena's hand dropped from his as he pulled away from her. She watched him head for the staircase. Taking a deep breath, she followed him into the entryway. She called after him. "You haven't once mentioned what happened last night."

Carter stopped at the top of the stairs. He turned slightly to see her face. "You didn't either."

She supposed he was right. When neither of them said

anything else, he finally turned away and went to his bedroom. She stood there for a few minutes after he closed the door.

Chapter Eight

Carter sipped his champagne and had to consciously stop himself from tugging at the bow tie on his tux. He had to admit he looked pretty good. The suit fit him well. The jacket sat evenly across his shoulders. And the holster, where he had his gun discreetly hidden, even fit under the material. The tailor had told him it was all in the cut that made the suit, and Carter took him at his word.

Carter had even taken a little extra time in the bathroom. He'd been extra careful with his razor, and he had even put a little pomade in his hair to tame it, though he wasn't convinced the product hadn't expired. When he'd come downstairs to fetch Selena, who had surprisingly been ready before him, from her office he'd been glad he had. Her eyes had widened a bit, and she'd given him a huge smile. She didn't smile much, at least not real ones, so he felt the effort well worth it.

Selena looked amazing. She favored cream colors or soft pastels. The dress this evening was cream-colored and draped her body perfectly. He could see shimmery threads woven through the dress, but the effect was subtle. Instead of glittering garishly as many of the women in the room did, she shone. Tonight, the pixie had been replaced by a siren. He could see a hint of cleavage, though not too much. The slit on her left side exposed a good length of her thigh, but only sometimes. The dress was meant to tease and tantalize, not to be overtly sexual.

He had been nervous about taking her to this event. He'd walked over to check on Ellis and had been informed that nothing shy of tying her up would keep her from the charity ball. It had been tempting, but in the end, he had opted for subtlety. But Selena had been right about one thing; security was tight. He could spot dozens of men in black jackets watching the people mingle around the oversized ballroom. Just the jewelry alone that these people wore required armed guards.

Carter made another round of the room. He saw John schmoozing donors, along with Isabelle. Jack and Theo were at home, waiting anxiously for their baby to come. Selena had spent the entire evening so far greeting people while explaining the purpose of the foundation to those who were guests but not yet involved in the foundation.

He had learned a lot about The Heart's Way Foundation by listening to her. The foundation had innumerable resources that it used to help other charities get off the ground. At first, he thought the idea was silly. Why give money to someone to help them show someone else how to make money? But the foundation had helped pilot several charities, many of which had become very successful in their endeavors. And the charity had contacts across the country that could be accessed to help people in need. The foundation coordinated other people's efforts.

He had also learned the foundation was just as active in its charitable activities. Selena had personally helped with raising funds to update the city's parks and schools in struggling neighborhoods. She also helped the foundation fund daycare programs and after-school programs that kept those same kids off the streets while their parents worked.

Then there was the hospital work. Selena had donated enough cash to build an entirely new children's wing in the city's largest hospital. The foundation helped the hospital's foundation raise funds to help families pay their bills. He'd learned that about halfway through the night while she had been giving a speech. She had spoken passionately and eloquently about the foundation and the many needs it helped fulfill. And it seemed she wasn't shy about putting her money where her mouth was.

"Are you enjoying yourself?" Selena had snuck up behind Sullivan, who had been watching the crowd.

"It's quite the party. Ellis said nothing would have kept you from coming tonight. I see why." Carter picked up a glass of champagne from a passing waiter and handed it to Selena. He had been nursing the same glass for the past couple of hours.

Selena tucked her arm into his. "It's hard to explain, but I need to be here, and not just because I was speaking. I started donating money to the foundation when an employee of Jack's told me about it. She has a brother with physical and mental disabilities. She had needed help desperately, and The Heart's Way was the only place that agreed to help her. She's here tonight."

Carter watched as Selena waved to a dark-haired woman standing near the buffet table. It took a moment before the woman took notice. She carefully made her way through the crowd.

"Selena, it's so good to see you. I was hoping to get the chance to speak to you."

Selena hugged the other woman. "Lindsay, it's so good to see you. How are you doing?"

Lindsay glanced over at Carter, then back to Selena. "I'm good. My brother's good, too. He just got married."

"Married? That's wonderful. You must be so happy for him." Selena hugged her again.

"I am. I'm also happy for myself. He married my best friend. But I was hoping to see you so I could ask about Ellis. Don't let him know I asked, but how is he?"

Carter stood by their side while they chatted about Ellis's condition. The woman was about Selena's height, but the women were very different. The woman had olive-toned skin, with brunette hair cut in a pixie style. The woman also had vivid green eyes, though it was hard to tell beneath all the makeup she wore.

"I wanted to go see him when I heard, but I didn't want to intrude." Lindsay looked over at Carter again. "I take it you're his replacement."

Carter held out his hand. The woman's grip was firm, and he found himself smiling at her friendly expression. "Temporarily. But tonight, I'm Selena's date. Carter Sullivan."

Lindsay laughed. "It's nice to meet you, Carter. You're a step up from her usual dates."

Selena pretended offense. "Really, they're not that bad."

Lindsay laughed again, the sound musical. "Yes, they are, and you know it."

Selena nodded, then was serious again. "You should go

see him, Lindsay. I know he'd like to see you. Letting you go was the dumbest thing he ever did."

Lindsay disagreed. "He doesn't want to see me. We're just not meant to be. But I am relieved he's doing all right. I read in the papers about the gunshots and someone trying to kill you."

Selena once again wrapped her arm in Sullivan's. "Sullivan here and Jack have been trying to find out who. The man who shot Wallace is dead. I'll admit it was terrifying at the time."

"Still is, I imagine. You look pale and you've lost weight. I can send my masseur to your house."

"Thank you, but for now it's best if I keep visitors to a minimum."

Carter watched Selena and Lindsay chat a little longer. Then the other woman bid them goodnight. Carter guided Selena over to the buffet. She had yet to eat. "Her masseur?"

"She's really into massage and maintains a very holistic lifestyle. She's into teas and other natural products. I didn't know it when I met her, but she dated Wallace. Sometimes it seems like there are not many women who haven't. They were engaged years ago, and up until a few years ago, on-and-off lovers."

Carter glanced over to where Lindsay was gathering her coat and exiting the party. "So why did they break up?"

Selena's mouth tightened. "Wallace. He told me he wasn't the right man for her. Shortly after they began dating, Lindsay's parents were killed. She was only twenty-two, but she had to take in her brother. As I said, he has some physical and mental impairments. He's older than her by a couple of years, but he was seriously injured his first year as a rookie fireman. He'd been in a burning building when it caved in. The beam that fell on him broke his back. And it also dislodged his safety equipment. The other firemen were able to rescue him, but he had not been breathing when they found him. The lack of oxygen damaged part of his brain. He has a hard time doing things like tying his shoes or holding utensils. He also has a hard time remembering things. But he survived and healed from the injury and was able to walk again, so all in all, he was lucky."

Carter rubbed his shoulder where one of his old bullet wounds was. He, too, had been lucky. But it had been hard to believe that when it happened. "So Ellis dumped her when she took in her brother?"

"When I asked Wallace why he broke up with her, he said it was because of her brother. She knew her brother didn't like Wallace, so she hadn't wanted to get into a serious relationship with Wallace because of him. But Wallace can be charming and convinced her otherwise. Wallace said they were really happy until her brother made it his mission to break them up."

"It's hard to make things work when the family isn't on board. He must have made things pretty difficult." Carter handed Selena a plate of food when she didn't start fixing one herself.

She took the plate. "When she took in her brother, her brother was angry and difficult. Lindsay had been trying to get him into counseling when he'd been living with their parents. She started pushing him harder when he moved in with her. He still refused to go. It's why I was surprised to hear he got married. I can't imagine any woman wanting to marry a man so angry and bitter."

She paused for a moment, then continued. "Anyway, the story goes that when her brother found out about her relationship with Wallace, he got really upset. Called her a lot of nasty names I won't repeat. When Lindsay continued to defend her brother's behavior, Wallace couldn't take it anymore. He, in a moment of stupidity, told her it was him or her brother."

"And Lindsay chose her brother."

"According to Wallace, Lindsay told him her brother needed her. She also said Wallace didn't." Selena took a few bites.

"You look thoughtful." Carter led her toward a sitting area.

"I should hire Lindsay's masseur to come help Wallace. His hands are like magic. He would get him healthy again in no time. Lindsay wouldn't be able to stay away."

"You're not seriously considering playing matchmaker, are you?" Carter was truly surprised by her. She didn't strike him as the sentimental type.

"They've been broken up for almost ten years, but Lindsay still cares about him. Wallace goes through women like water and won't commit to any of them. And every year when he sees her at the foundation's annual charity ball, his eyes follow her."

Carter just shook his head. "Don't worry about Ellis's love life. If he wanted her, he would have gone after her. Like you said, he's not shy."

Selena sighed and let it go. "I suppose. I need to go to the ladies' room."

Carter came to her side to escort her.

"Seriously, Sullivan, I don't need you to follow me to the bathroom. It's perfectly safe." Selena handed him her plate.

He knew she had a point. He had already scoped out the entire ballroom and the corridors that led to the bathrooms. She would be perfectly fine. Not to mention all the people coming and going.

Selena lifted her skirt a bit as she wound her way through the crowd. She knew Sullivan was following at a discreet distance but didn't look like he was going to insist on coming with her all the way. In that way, he operated the same as Wallace. He would keep a slight distance between them but was never too far out of reach should she need him.

Selena greeted a few people on her way to the hall. She opened one of the double doors. The ladies' room was at the end of the hall. Smaller meeting rooms that were currently unoccupied lined one side of the hall. In the washroom, she greeted a few other women who were freshening up their makeup. When Selena was finished, she touched up her lipstick and powdered her face.

The hall was empty when she left the ladies' room. She was halfway back to the double doors when a large hand shot out of one of the meeting rooms to grab her. She started to scream when another large hand clamped over her mouth. She tried to fight off the man who grabbed her, but he was much stronger than she was. The man slammed her up against the wall. In a daze, she slid to the floor. Her vision swam a little, but she could make out a large man holding a gun.

"You make this too easy, Selena." The large man nodded to a second man waiting in the shadows.

The second man came toward her. She would have screamed, but the man hit her in the jaw with the gun he was holding.

"Be still."

The second man tore a strip of duct tape from the roll he was holding. She tried to get away from him, but she was backed up against the wall. She felt tears fall as the man covered her mouth with tape.

"Now her arms and feet. But don't tie her feet too tight." The large man commanded the second.

In short order, Selena found her arms jerked in front of her and her wrists tied together. The man then bound her feet, but she would still be able to walk, though in a short shuffle.

"I should end this now." The large man came toward her and jerked her to her feet.

Selena whimpered when the man kissed the tape that covered her mouth. He pressed the gun to her temple.

"But some sense of perversity has me wanting to make the game last a little longer. You should have died at the hands of a crazed gunman. It seemed like a fitting end for you, my dear. But that bulldog of a bodyguard had to spoil my fun."

Selena's tears were now falling down her cheeks. Her jaw hurt where he'd struck her, and her temple hurt from hitting the wall. The gun was pressed up against the cut she had gotten during the gun attack at her office.

The large man grabbed the roll of tape from the other man. "Now I see you've replaced him. Carter Sullivan, ex-cop. Not sure if that's a step up or a step down. What do you think he'll do when he finds you? He'll probably want to lock you away in that monstrosity of a house you keep. And what of your friends? Do you think they'll even care if I were to just shoot you now? Jack and Theo are too busy with their impending parenthood to care. John and Isabelle are too busy trying to hose people out of their hard-earned money. Or how about Wallace's ex, the brunette you were just talking to? She'll be glad to have the competition out of the way. And Wallace will just be glad you didn't get him shot again."

Selena trembled wildly as the man tore a few strips of tape off the roll. He spun her around, pushing her to walk deeper into the shadows of the room. He then used the tape to anchor her arms above her head on a large light fixture hanging on the wall. She felt his hands on her body, working her dress up to her waist. The gun was now pressed into her belly as the man wrapped his arms around her. She tried to fight him, but he just laughed in her ear. "Keep fighting me. It just makes it that much better."

Voices outside in the hallway had the large man stopping. His hands stopped just shy of the prize he sought. "Take a look."

The second man went to the door. "We need to go. Her boyfriend is looking for her."

Selena's head exploded in pain, then nothing.

* * *

Carter found himself extremely annoyed as he waited near the hallway doors for Selena to get back from the bathroom. She'd probably stopped to redo her makeup. Not that she needed to. The woman without makeup was simply stunning.

He gave her another two minutes, then he'd had it. He pushed through the double doors. All of the meeting room doors had been locked earlier in the night. The only doors that were unlocked were the bathrooms.

Carter stopped the woman who left the bathroom. "Sorry to bother you, but was my date in there? Petite blonde, wearing a cream dress?"

The woman gave him a cheery look. He realized she was inebriated. She giggled and shook her head. "No one is in there, but I wouldn't be opposed to going back in if you come with me."

Carter had to take a couple of steps back as the woman tried to latch onto him. "Thanks for the offer, but I'm with someone."

The woman pouted but let him go. She made her way back to the ballroom, where he had no doubt she'd find herself a date for the night.

Carter stepped into the ladies' bathroom, but it was indeed empty. Trying to keep calm, he left the room. He grabbed his phone and sent an emergency text to John. In less than a minute, the other man was in the hall.

"Selena's disappeared. I need you to alert security and make sure no one leaves the building."

John pulled a comm device from his pocket. "Put the building on lockdown. No one comes in, and no one goes out."

John pulled the hotel's master key card out of his pocket. "We'll start with these rooms."

Carter pulled his gun and waited until John had the door undone. He went in low. Lights automatically came on. He went further into the room. He could hear John in the room next door. He opened cabinets large enough to hold a body and a closet. Carter shouted into the hall. "She's not in here."

"Not here." John met Carter back in the hall and opened two more rooms. Carter went into the one. He heard a shout and a slam from the hall.

Carter ran from the room. He saw John holding his nose where a door had been slammed against his face. From the corner of his eye, he saw two men in tuxedos go through the double doors. He gave chase. Carter shouted to John as he followed the two men. "See if she's in there."

Carter shoved through the double doors and realized there was no way he was going to find the men. The room was a sea of black tuxedos and evening dresses. He questioned a few people if they had seen where the men went, but no one had.

Carter went back through the doors. He heard John's voice talking softly. He found John holding Selena. She was dangling from the wall.

"Do you have a knife? We need to cut the tape off." John was still crooning to Selena, who was still in his arms.

Carter pulled a large pocketknife from his trouser pocket

and his cell phone from the other. "Hold her up."

"What are you doing?" John watched in disbelief as Carter took a picture.

"Evidence. Now hold her up while I cut her loose." Carter sliced through the tape on her hands, then went to her feet. While John held her, he pulled the tape from her mouth as gently as he could. Her skin was red where he'd removed it.

Carter transferred Selena from John's arms to his. "Call Detective Quinlan. Have him send an ambulance."

John grabbed his cell phone and dialed.

Carter carefully carried her to a cushioned bench. It wouldn't be comfortable, but it was the best he could do. "Come on, baby. Wake up for me."

Carter saw fresh marks on Selena's face and temple. The bastards had hit her multiple times. Trying not to panic, but truly scared, Carter took off his jacket and wrapped it around her.

"Mac is on his way, along with an ambulance. Has she moved?" John dropped to his knees beside Carter.

"No. She's out. Go make sure your wife is safe, and then bring back some ice. I can at least try to keep the swelling down."

Carter held Selena's hand and kept up a steady stream of conversation. She opened her eyes a few times, but he couldn't get her to stay awake. John returned with Isabelle in tow. He handed Carter a towel with ice.

"She opened her eyes, but she's still not conscious. Please go wait by the doors for the ambulance." Carter's voice was hoarse.

John took Isabelle's hand and led her from the room. Within a few minutes, they returned with the detective and the paramedics. Security was keeping the guests out of the hallway. Carter was pretty sure the men who attacked her would have slipped out by now, but he hoped the security cameras would give them a good visual of the men.

Carter answered the questions Mac shot at him while explaining to the paramedics that Selena had just recovered from a previous concussion. Her vitals were steady, and she was responding to stimuli. Between questions, Carter held her hand, urging her to wake up. Ignoring both John and Mac, Carter followed the paramedics as they took her to the hospital.

"We'll meet you there in a few." John held Isabelle against him.

Mac pulled his keys from his pocket. "I'll drive. I'm guessing you two have been drinking."

Isabelle gave him a watery laugh. "Yeah, we probably should get a ride. Wouldn't want to have to make you arrest us."

Mac ushered the couple out to his vehicle and drove them to the hospital, keeping pace behind the ambulance.

Chapter Nine

Selena woke up in a hospital bed; her head and face hurt, and she was disoriented. Panic set in. "Sullivan!"

Carter shot up out of his seat. "I'm right here."

Her head turned toward his voice. She started pulling at the blood pressure cuff and IV as tears streamed down her cheeks.

Carter stilled her arms and pulled her against him. His heart broke when her arms came around him and she started sobbing against his chest. He shifted so he could sit on the bed and hold her while she wept.

Selena's tears didn't last long. She began to realize where she was. She was safe. Sullivan had found her. The men who attacked her couldn't hurt her anymore.

When the tears abated, he released her. He grabbed the cup of water that had been left for her and let her have a few sips. "I need you to tell me what happened."

Selena's wet eyes glanced up at Sullivan; then she saw the detective standing in the doorway, along with Isabelle and John. "I don't..."

Carter brushed her bangs back from her forehead. "I'm right here with you. I swear I won't let anything else happen to you."

Selena's face crumpled. "It was my fault. I told you not to come with me. I just needed to go to the bathroom. I felt safe. I've been at that hotel dozens of times. I was coming out of the bathroom. I was on my way back when I was grabbed from behind. He pulled me into a room, then slammed me against the wall. When I looked up from the floor, the man had a gun. I was so scared, and he hit me when I tried to scream. All I could think was that this time there was no one to save me."

Carter took her hand but prodded her on. "How many men were there?"

Selena closed her eyes. "There were two. The large man told the other man to tie me up. He taped my arms and legs and taped my mouth. The large man then taped me to the light fixture. He was going to rape me."

Carter let the rage he felt course through his system for a moment. Then he got himself back under control. "What did he say to you?"

"He said he should end this now. But then he said since I survived the shooting, he'd decided to enjoy the game. Then he said no one would care if he shot me."

Carter began to worry when her eyes closed again, but then the pressure of her grip on his hand suddenly increased.

Selena's eyes shot open, and she struggled to sit up. "He knows me. He knows everyone's names. He knows Jack and Theo are expecting a baby. He knows Isabelle and John are fundraising. He even knows Lindsay dated Wallace."

"What else?" Carter tipped her chin up so he could look into her eyes when she went silent.

"He knows you. He knows your name and the fact that you used to be a cop. He called Wallace a bulldog and called you his replacement."

Mac came further into the room. "Do you know him?"

Selena shook her head. "I don't know. He was wearing a mask; both men were. The men were whispering, so it was hard to hear them. I was just too scared."

Mac came around to the other side of her bed. "The man on the camera was not quite six feet. Brunette. We got a good shot of the shorter man, the second man. He blocked the view of the taller man, who kept his head down. There's no way to identify him. White, six feet, brunette. That's all we've got."

"The taller one is the one who wants me dead. The second man was just a lookout. The larger man had come up behind me, grabbed my skirt, and told me he liked it when I fought him. Then he heard voices. I think he hit me then. I don't remember anything else."

Mac patted her free hand. "Good news is you remember something. After a blow to the head, it's not uncommon for people not to remember anything. The doctor said it was more shock than the blow that caused you to pass out. He doesn't believe you have a concussion this time."

Selena pressed her face into Carter's chest. "I want to go home."

"I know, baby, but you need to stay the night for observation. I'll be with you the whole time."

Mac took a step back. "We're questioning the guests, but I don't expect to find much. The crowd was a little drunk and having too good a time to notice anything bad happening. I'll start running some facial recognition on the second man. Maybe we'll get lucky."

Selena looked up briefly. "Thank you, Detective. And if

any of my people can be of assistance in your search, please let McCray know."

"I certainly will, Miss Powell. You get some rest."

"Can we get you anything?" Isabelle took the spot that the detective had vacated.

Selena nodded her head and continued to lean up against Sullivan, who had his arms wrapped securely around her. "You'll need to let Wallace know what happened. He'll have the house under surveillance while we are out. He'll worry when we don't return."

John stepped further into the room. "I called him a few minutes ago. We assured him you're fine. He was ready to drive out here, but I talked him out of it."

"Thank you, John. He needs to rest."

Carter piped in. "So do you."

Selena relaxed a little more. She suddenly felt extremely tired. "And don't tell Daniel. There's nothing he can do, and I don't want to upset him."

"He won't hear it from me." Carter eased her down and tucked the covers up to her chin.

Isabelle's phone beeped, and she checked it. "I didn't want to say anything earlier, but Theo went into labor while we were at the ball. She's up in maternity now."

Selena felt a healing burst of happiness, along with a brief burst of energy. "How exciting. I know she's been anxious for this baby to come."

John came and wrapped his arm around his wife's waist. "We're going to head over there and keep Jack company. Theo's dad is on his way, and his wife and baby are going to come in a few hours."

"Call me as soon as he's here." Selena relaxed against the pillow, keeping Sullivan's hand in hers.

"We will." Isabelle kissed Selena's forehead.

Carter left her side and dimmed the lights. "You really should rest. You've had a shock."

Selena's eyes felt droopy. She did not doubt that whatever the medication was in the IV, it was meant to calm and relax her. "It's so nice about Jack and Theo. The perfect ending to an awful day."

"Close your eyes now."

"You'll stay with me?"

Carter pulled up a reclining chair next to the bed. "I'll be right here all night."

That made Selena smile. "What's left of it. It's almost morning."

"The sooner it comes, the sooner you can go home." Carter kicked up the footrest. He needed to close his eyes, too. He had one of Selena's security guards outside the door. He would remain there until they left. He also had an escort ready and waiting. They'd have two SUVs with armed men taking them back to Selena's home. After tonight, he was taking no more chances. And after tonight, he knew with absolute certainty there was still someone out there who wanted Selena dead.

* * *

The medication helped Selena sleep through the rest of the night and into the morning. The doctor came around eleven and told her he was releasing her. It was another two hours before she was finally discharged. She was startled by the group of men waiting outside the hospital for them, but she didn't say anything. And she didn't insist she drive. Sullivan drove them home in a borrowed SUV. One of the men would drive it back. Her Mercedes was still at the hotel. Sullivan told her he wanted to have it looked over for tampering before he retrieved it. Selena had visions of car bombs going off and didn't argue. After what she had been through, she would let Sullivan be overprotective.

She thanked the men and undid the alarm. She tossed her purse on the sideboard, not bothering to put it in her office where she normally did. She headed for the kitchen.

"Have a seat, Selena. I'll fix you something. What do you want?"

Selena dropped her head into her hands. "Just some water. I don't know what medication they doped me up with, but I feel like I haven't had a drink in days."

Carter went to the fridge and pulled out a bottle of sparkling water. He handed it to her after taking the cap off. He watched her down half the bottle. "You should rest."

Selena shook her head. "I just want to sit here."

Carter wasn't sure what to make of her mood. He was hungry himself and hoped maybe he could get her to eat. While he went about fixing lunch, he struggled for a neutral topic of conversation. He latched onto the first one he thought of.

"I never asked, but how many brothers or sisters do you have?" He didn't know much about Daniel's relationship with Selena, other than she was his aunt. He remembered Ellis mentioning a brother and sister, but she wouldn't know that. And since he had a growing desire to know more about her, starting with her family seemed like a good place to start.

Selena glanced up, a bit confused by the random question, but willing to answer him. Anything to break the silence stretching between them. "I have one of each. My mom was married before my dad, but he died young. They're twins. Samuel and Samantha."

"Seriously? Sam and Sam?"

Selena gave him a real smile. "My mom was Sylvia. Her mother was Sally. Then I came and was Selena."

"Your dad didn't mind?"

"My dad didn't want children, so he didn't much care what she called me. They got married because he needed someone with class and money who could add legitimacy to his failing antiquities business. She gave him that. I was an accident. He would rather she had ended the pregnancy, but whatever her reasons were, she decided to keep me."

"Are you close to your brother and sister? You seem close to Daniel."

Selena sat back, too tired to question his sudden interest. "We're not close. My sister thinks Daniel was switched at birth, and she doesn't have much to do with him. It doesn't seem to faze him. As for me, they don't like me because they don't like my father. Not that I can blame them. Our mother was much older when she had me, so we aren't close in age. I haven't seen them since our mother's funeral almost eight years ago. They disliked my father so much they didn't want our mother's share of the business she'd kept after their divorce. They wanted me to sell the shares, but instead, we compromised. They kept the house and all her personal effects, and I kept the business shares instead. In hindsight, it wasn't one of my better ideas."

He found that statement odd, given that their current surroundings were paid for by said business. "You've made the business a huge success. I'd say you made the right decision."

Selena turned her head away from him, needing a moment to regroup. She couldn't explain to him that her father and husband had tried to murder her. He hadn't lived here when it happened, and since he didn't travel in her social circles, he didn't know. And she couldn't tell him that by taking the business, she'd severed what little relationship she had with her brother and sister. They felt she was picking sides, and it wasn't theirs.

What she really didn't want to tell him was how much she lived in fear; fear of her own making. She kept fortress walls around her, and a bodyguard ever-present. She tried to right the wrongs she saw around her every day in the hope that one day the fear would fade. In the six years since her father had been locked up and her husband killed, she had yet to shake the feeling that she wasn't safe. Should she have gone to a therapist, he probably would have told her she needed to accept what had happened to her and move on. Instead, she had built walls, both figuratively and literally, around her to protect herself. Carter Sullivan was the first man who made her want to tear them down, or at least let him inside.

But even with the fortress walls around her, the large man had stolen her sense of security. He showed her that for all her efforts, all the money she spent, it could be demolished in a single moment. The past six years of solitude had been for nothing. She was as vulnerable now as she had been six years ago.

Carter didn't like the look on her face. Her skin was pale, the bruises more prominent than they had been a moment ago. "Come back to me, Selena."

Selena heard Sullivan calling to her, and she brought herself back to the present. They were talking about her family. "What about you? Brothers or sisters?"

Relieved that she was alert again, he answered. "I have a sister. She lives on the east coast. She keeps trying to get me to move out there. She and her husband moved to New York a few years back when she got a promotion and a transfer at work. They have four boys."

Selena drank some more of her water. "Do you want to go?"

Carter shook his head. "Not really. I thought about it after I quit, but I own my own home, and I felt like if I left, then I was giving up. And honestly, I don't want to give up California weather and trade it in for snowy winters. Plus, I don't have the cash."

Selena rested her chin on her hands. "You have the money now. I know how much I'm paying you."

Carter set their lunch on the table. "Let's just say I'm not an East Coast kind of guy."

Selena felt her lips kick up into a small smile. "Now that I believe. Are your parents still alive?"

"No. My dad died of a heart attack when I was a rookie. My mom died of cancer when I was just a little kid."

"I'm sorry, Sullivan. That must have been hard." Selena looked at the plate, but there was no way she was eating anything.

"No more so for me than for you. You lost both of your parents."

Selena didn't correct him. Her father might not be dead, but he was lost to her. Instead of dwelling on it, she watched as Sullivan ate what was on his plate.

"Please eat something." Carter pushed a plate of sliced melon in front of her.

Her stomach revolted. She pushed herself off the stool and ran to the bathroom.

Carter quickly followed. He stood outside the door, and his heart broke a little as he listened to her retching. "I'm coming in."

Selena's head hung limply over the bowl. She didn't care that Sullivan had followed, or that she normally would be feeling extremely embarrassed. She let him help her to her feet. She grabbed a toothbrush she kept downstairs and brushed the foul taste out of her mouth. She didn't argue when he carried her up the stairs and settled her on her bed.

"Stay. Please?" Selena felt her eyes closing, even though she didn't want to fall asleep for fear of the dreams that might follow.

Carter didn't have the heart to leave her alone. He tucked her under the covers, then lay down beside her. She sought the warmth of his body. Though he couldn't help the sudden desire that hit him as he lay in her bed, he kept his hands above the covers.

Carter didn't leave her bed. Selena lay asleep next to him

for the next two hours. When she stirred, it was a little after five.

When Selena opened her eyes, she saw Sullivan watching her. She could see heat in his gaze. The look had her insides thawing. She'd been feeling numb since she woke up this morning. But right now, she felt anything but.

"Feel better?"

Selena nodded, unable to speak. She lifted her hand to his cheek. She wanted to draw him closer to her, to taste what she had yet to taste.

Carter pulled away. He wasn't sure of his self-control. Given all that had happened since he'd met her, once he touched her, there would be no going back. "Don't."

Selena watched wide-eyed as he got up from the bed. He was halfway to the door when she climbed out of bed. "Sullivan, I…"

Carter cut her off. "My name is Carter, Selena. I want you to say it."

Selena knew what he wanted. He had asked her before when he wasn't sober enough to realize what he was asking her. But he knew what he was asking her now. He wanted her to let go of the past; to acknowledge what was between them. Both of them had been keeping their distance, and he was asking her to break down that barrier. She opened her mouth, but nothing came out. Helplessly she watched as his eyes became remote.

Carter took a step back from her and looked into her eyes. He needed her to surrender to him. It may be just getting her to say his name, but it was important. He needed to know that he meant something to her. That she could put her barriers aside and focus on just him. With other women, desire would have been enough. But with Selena, he wanted more. When she remained silent, when he saw nothing of what she felt in her gaze, he turned away from her to leave the room.

Selena felt painful, strong emotions for the first time in a long time when he turned his back on her. He made her feel more than any man had before. And she was frightened, not only of what he wanted from her but of what she wanted to give him. Before she could find an excuse, she opened her mouth to say his name. She couldn't bear for him to walk away from her again.

"Carter." His name came out barely a whisper.

He turned back to her. He could see a sheen of tears in her eyes. He crossed back to her, cupping her chin in his hand. Without hesitation, he took her mouth with his. The taste of her was indescribable, yet oddly familiar. Her mouth opened under his. He dragged her body closer, pressing her curves against him. She went stiff for a moment, then seemed to liquefy against him. He released her face, instead cupping her hips to keep her upright.

Selena wound her arms around Carter's neck, needing the strength of his body to keep her from falling. Her knees had gone weak when he'd clasped her body up against the hard planes and angles of his. The first feel of his arousal against her lower belly caused all of the strength in her body to leave. She had never felt this way before. She was the strong one, the one who kept everything together. Carter made her vulnerable, dependent on him. It was both arousing and frightening at the same time.

There wasn't much finesse to their lovemaking. Carter, knowing he should slow down, couldn't seem to stop rushing to the finish. The first taste of her drove him mad. She was clinging to him as if she'd never let go. He plunged his tongue into her mouth again and again, dragging her toward the bed.

Selena was wearing her gown from the night before. Carter still wore his tuxedo. She watched helplessly as he stripped off his clothes until he was completely nude before her. What had been a small ache became a painful longing. At first, it was his arousal that held her attention. What she saw made her nervous. She was a petite woman, and he was a large man. But then her gaze lifted, and she saw and touched the bullet wound in his left shoulder. Her nerves fell away as she touched first his old scar, then his new wound. She could only imagine the pain he had endured and was still enduring because of her. He hadn't worn the sling in days, and the temporary cast had been removed, but the healing flesh was a reminder of what had happened to him because of her.

"Does it bother you?" Carter's hands went to the fastening of her gown. He wanted to see her.

"No, it doesn't bother me." Her hands trailed to his belly, where a second scar marred the perfection of his muscular abdomen.

Not wanting to talk about it, he stripped Selena of her dress. He was so intent on what he was doing that he didn't notice the trembling in her hands as she touched him. She wasn't wearing a bra, and her underwear quickly joined the pile of clothing. When he finally had her naked, he took a moment to drink in the sight of her. Her breasts were tipped with pale pink nipples. Her belly had just the slightest hint of curve. His eyes drifted lower. He let his hands drift over what he had exposed. When he cupped her breasts, she arched into his touch. He let his fingers drift lower, enjoying the feel of her very curvy, very firm backside.

First his hands, then his mouth, found the flesh of her breasts. Selena clenched her hands on his forearms to keep her balance. When his teeth took one of her nipples into his mouth, she had to lock her knees to stay on her feet. Her hands trailed up his chest, finding his male nipples under the thick mat of hair. She scraped her nails over them and was rewarded when he shuddered under her hands.

Selena felt the room spin when Carter picked her up and set her on the bed. He left her for a moment and picked up his jacket. She saw a small packet in his hand. She watched him as he tore open the wrapper and rolled a condom on. She lay still as he came down on top of her, his weight pressing her body into the mattress. The feel of his body against hers was indescribable. She could feel the hair on his chest against her breasts. She could feel the thickness of his thighs as he slid between hers, his fingers finding the waiting warmth of her body.

Carter's breath was heaving, and he was struggling for control. It had been too long since he'd been with a woman, and because this was Selena he had under him, what was left of his sanity was fading fast.

Selena wrapped her arms around him. She could feel him probing at the entrance of her body. "Carter."

The breathy sound of his name from her lips shredded what was left of his control. "I can't take this slow. Not this first time."

Selena felt him surge into her body. Her immediate reaction was not pleasure, but a burning pain. She stiffened underneath him, her nails digging into the muscles of his back.

Despite his rush, he couldn't help but feel the sudden tension in her body. She had her eyes closed, and her nails were digging painfully into his back. He held himself still for a moment. "Selena?"

She opened her eyes to see the concern in his. She said the first thing that came to mind. "It hurts."

Carter cursed. When that just made her tense, he simply lay still. Nowhere in his mind had it occurred to him that she might be a virgin. "You need to relax your body. Let it adjust to mine."

Selena did as he told her. His soft words in her ear told her how beautiful she was and how much he wanted her, making her body relax.

He braced himself above her on his good arm, his other hand brushing the hair back from her forehead. He then bent to kiss her, this time taking the time to fully enjoy the moment. His body was demanding he finish what he started, but he wanted Selena with him. He found her breasts once more and teased them until she arched her back to increase the pressure of his touch, his mouth never leaving hers.

Selena completely relaxed as Carter kissed her and caressed her body. She was once again in the moment, her fingers now buried in the dark depths of his hair, her tongue tangled with his. She then felt his fingers drift to where their bodies were joined. His touch teased and tormented her. She found herself trying to bring their bodies closer.

Carter teased her until he couldn't take it anymore. Still braced above her, he slowly began to move inside her. He now used his hand to guide her hips, pulling her thigh higher. She instinctively tightened herself around him, her thighs gripping his body as tightly as she could. His words encouraged her to move with him.

For Selena, what pain she had felt was now being replaced with the pleasure she had known she would find with Carter. She could feel him surging into her, the rhythm of their bodies straining toward release. Her breath was coming in pants, and her fingers were now gripping his waist, trying to pull him deeper inside. She could feel her lower body tightening around his. She strained to get even closer.

Carter kissed her again, his breath coming as fast as hers, no longer able to speak. He could feel the desperate clenching of Selena's body around him, but she wasn't quite there. Knowing he wasn't going to last much longer, he slid his hand back between their bodies and used his fingers to push her over the edge.

At the first touch of Carter's hand, she felt the incredible tension that had built inside her shatter. She held him tightly as her first climax rolled over her. All she could do was say his name and hold on.

Carter felt the clenching of her body. He kept his fingers on her, prolonging her pleasure, as he followed her over the edge. He surged one last time into her, and he had to grit his teeth to keep from shouting his release into the darkness of the bedroom.

For a time, all Selena could hear was their breathing. Carter was lax on top of her, his entire body resting against hers. Her body was still pulsing slightly from inside. Her body was also completely relaxed, her thighs now resting against him.

Carter groaned and pulled out of her. He heard Selena's slight gasp as he did. He glanced down, and she had a small smile on her lips. He kissed her lightly, then climbed to his feet. He was surprised at how weak his legs felt.

Selena opened her eyes to see his retreating body. She saw him go to the bathroom, then come back, minus the condom. She blushed but didn't say anything. He climbed back into her bed.

Carter pulled Selena on top of him, and he let out the breath he had been holding when she laid her head on his chest, her body completely relaxed. "You should have said something."

Selena didn't answer; instead, she kissed his chin, then pressed her lips to the curve of his neck.

They lay quietly for a time. Then the long night and day caught up with both of them, and they fell asleep once more.

Chapter Ten

Carter woke after midnight. He knew immediately Selena wasn't in the bed any longer. He lay there for a moment, looking up at the ceiling. He was still amazed at the connection he felt to her, a woman he would never have believed had any passion inside her.

As he lay still, he heard music playing. The sound was faint, but because he was a music lover, he could make out some of the melodies. If he wasn't mistaken, someone was playing the piano. The music didn't sound recorded. He pulled on his boxers and left Selena's bedroom.

Carter followed the sound of the song to the music room. Selena was seated at the piano, wearing nothing but his tuxedo shirt. He felt his loins swell at the sight of her, but it was the music that held his attention. The melody was haunting, as if the writer had poured their soul into the song. He could hear the pain in the notes she played, but there was something underneath the pain. The pain drifted away as the song progressed, and the song ended with hope.

"You said you didn't play." Carter leaned against the doorjamb, much as Selena had the day she found him playing. She began playing another piece.

She glanced up at him without missing a note. "I said I didn't play, not that I couldn't. I can't remember the last time I sat here and played. I used to spend hours behind this piano. It belonged to my grandmother. She taught me how to play."

Carter entered the room. "Do you know how to play the other instruments that you have in here?"

"Some. I was always best on the piano, though I can play most stringed instruments. I have a flute tucked away that belonged to my great-grandmother in the bench seat by the window, but I was never good with woodwind or brass instruments. And you don't want to hear me play percussion."

"I don't know this song, but it's beautiful." He took a few more steps toward her.

Selena glanced up again but didn't respond. Her slender fingers were sure and nimble across the keys. Her skill greatly surpassed his own.

Carter took a seat next to her on the piano bench. He couldn't help but feel pleased when she missed a note as his thigh brushed hers. He looked up at the sheet music in front of her. The song title simply said 'untitled'. He took a closer look and realized the music was handwritten on the page. "You wrote this?"

She stopped playing and tucked her hands in her lap. She looked at Carter, who had an incredulous look on his face. "I wrote this. I was barely twenty, I think."

Carter touched her cheek with his fingers. Something else occurred to him. This wasn't a hobby he was hearing. He rose from the piano bench and headed to the window seat. He lifted the padded wooden bench. Inside it were reams and reams of staff paper. He picked up the first pile. All the sheets were handwritten. He hummed a few of the notes.

Selena sat completely still, feeling completely exposed, even more exposed than when she had stood naked before him. She watched as he walked back toward her. He set two sheets of staff paper on the piano. Without him asking, she began to play. This song was written when she'd met Jack. Despite the craziness of what was going on in her life, Jack had managed to pull a few laughs from her. The song was lighthearted, a little jaunty. If the song had lyrics, she imagined they would be, too. He had kissed her for the first time the day she wrote this, though she knew when he did, they were not destined for a great romance. But the kiss, so sweet and tender, had eased the ache in her heart and allowed her to feel a bit of peace and happiness.

Carter went back to the bench and pulled another song from the stack. She played it in its entirety. The music could have been the background to a ghost story or a gothic novel. The music was not peaceful; it bordered on angry yet was brooding at the same time.

"So many emotions you put into music. Yet so little you show others." Carter took her chin in his hand.

"It's easier to express them in music."

"I think you try to purge them from you, so you won't have to feel them." Carter sat beside her once again, pulling her suddenly rigid body against him.

Selena gave in to him and relaxed, wrapping her arms around his naked waist, her naked thigh pressed against his. She rubbed her cheek against the hair on his chest, loving the feel of it against her skin.

"Why don't you play professionally? It's obvious from

the stacks of music how much you love it." Carter brushed his cheek against the top of her head.

Selena pressed a kiss to his chest. "I wanted to. But what I really wanted to do was be a lounge singer, singing my own songs."

That got a chuckle out of Carter. "A lounge singer, huh? Do you sing?"

Selena extracted herself from his arms and went to the bookcase. She pulled out a notebook. "I was never as good with lyrics as I was with melody, which is why I never would have made it as a lounge singer, at least not singing my own songs. I tried, but I never seemed to get the words right. I met a girl when I was in music school. She was studying voice and ballet. She was also a songwriter. She asked me if she could write lyrics for some of my songs."

Carter scooted over to give her plenty of room to play. He saw the sheet music had handwritten lyrics on them. She began to play, her voice joining the piano. He stood and looked down at her. Her melodious soprano joined the notes she drew from the piano, a contrast to her low, sexy speaking voice. Her voice dipped and rose; she held the higher-pitched lyrics as if she were born to sing. When the song ended, he stood there without words.

She closed the notebook and closed the lid of the piano. "You might be the first person to hear me sing since school. I haven't sung a single note in public for over six years."

Carter found his voice. "Why? Words can't begin to describe how your music moved me."

Selena felt tears gather and her throat constrict. This man, this hard yet beautiful man, drew feelings from her she had never felt before. "I never wanted to give up music, but I did the year my mom died. I thought there were good reasons at the time."

Carter just shook his head, unable to understand what could have been more important than the music she so obviously loved. "What reasons?"

"It's a little complicated. But I suppose I should tell you about my husband before I get into the reasons. But I'd like to eat first."

Husband? "But you were a virgin."

Selena turned her back to him and headed to the kitchen. "He's part of the reason why."

Carter followed. Selena opened the fridge and pulled out a carton of milk. She then went to the cabinet and pulled out a couple of bowls, a couple of spoons, and a box of cereal. A bit perplexed by her sudden mood, he sat at the island and watched her pour two bowls.

"I can't tell you the last time I ate a bowl of cereal. Oatmeal maybe, but not cold cereal." Carter pulled the bowl toward him but didn't add milk.

Selena drowned her cereal in milk and took a bite. "I don't think I've seen you eat breakfast once since you got here, other than that slice of toast the other day."

Shaking his head, Carter poured a little milk over his cereal and took a bite. The cereal wasn't as sweet as the cereals he remembered eating as a kid. "I usually drink half a pot of coffee for breakfast and grab an early lunch."

They sat quietly side by side at the island, eating their cereal. Selena poured a second smaller bowl and drowned that one as well. When they were both finished, she rinsed the dishes and set them in the dishwasher. She put away the milk before once again facing Carter.

"My husband's name was Carter McGrath. He owned a courier service. He had a contract with my father. My dad wanted to merge the two businesses but didn't want to lose control of what was his. I had gone to work with my father the year before, and my dad had this great idea that if I married McGrath, then we could combine the businesses and keep them in the family, or so he said. My mother, who had owned half the company, had just died the year before. As I mentioned before, my brother and sister took everything else, and I took her shares. I owned half the company, and my dad was not happy about it."

Carter interrupted. "Your husband's name was Carter?"

She nodded. "He wasn't exactly what you would call marrying material. He was sleeping with half the women in town. He wasn't picky. But part of what my dad said rang true. The company was on the brink of failure, and little of what I was trying to do was pulling it back from the brink. McGrath's business had a huge cash reserve. I suggested we simply merge the two companies. My dad refused unless there was a wedding. I agreed to a marriage of convenience to expedite the merger. The only reason I agreed was because I didn't want to see the business my grandfather had built ruined. Nowhere in the agreement did it say I had to stay married to him. McGrath didn't find our separate bedrooms convenient, but he eventually stopped trying to talk me into bed."

"You refused to sleep with him because of all the other women he was sleeping with." Carter knew without question that she wouldn't be one to share.

"Yes. He said he'd quit seeing them, but I wasn't that naive or stupid. Shortly after we married, I was almost killed in a car accident. My brake lines went out. I took the car to a mechanic and had them fixed without question. Then there was an occasion when I almost fell off the balcony of our penthouse apartment. It seemed one of the rails had come loose."

Carter came off the stool. The cop in him put two and two together. "He tried to kill you."

She simply nodded again and continued with her story. "Then there was a box that almost fell on my head at work. It no longer seemed coincidental. At no point did I alert my husband or my father that I realized what had been happening. Instead, I hired a private investigator."

"That's how you met Jack." Carter paced the large kitchen.

"Yes, that's how I met Jack. He looked into my husband. He wasn't able to find evidence against him. But he did find something."

Carter stopped pacing. "What?"

"My father had a life insurance policy out on me. And Jack told me that if I were to die without a will, my husband would inherit my half of the company. They'd not only get a fat cash payout at my accidental death, but they would own the company in full between the two of them."

"What happened to them?"

Selena took a deep breath. "Jack found enough evidence against my father. He's currently serving a twenty-year sentence. McGrath was killed in a plane crash."

"Seems convenient."

"Believe me, I was immensely relieved. He had disappeared when my father was arrested, and Jack was trying to find him. I was living in fear that he would find me. I asked Jack to find me a bodyguard, one who could dig into people's lives. Had I known how, I could have found the plan my father and McGrath had concocted. Jack sent me Wallace, who, as you know, is not only an excellent bodyguard but also a computer hacker. He helped me erase any record of my marriage. I destroyed all physical documents, and Wallace erased them from public records."

Carter pulled a shaking Selena into his arms. He wasn't sure she even realized she was trembling. He pressed her face to his chest. "I won't even ask how Ellis accomplished that. But how does Jack know he was killed in a plane crash?"

Selena burrowed closer. "McGrath was a pilot. That's how he got into the courier business. Jack had his plane under surveillance and had sabotaged the plane to make it unsafe to fly. The sabotage was obvious, but McGrath took off anyway when Jack and his men tried to confront him. The plane was found, crashed and burned, along with McGrath's body in the pilot's seat."

The house, the bodyguard, her reserve, it all made sense. And it was no wonder she didn't trust anyone, especially men. She might have been able to overcome her husband trying to kill her. But he bet her father trying to kill her was much more traumatizing. He wondered why John and Jack hadn't told him about her husband. They had been open about her father.

Then a thought struck him. Despite what she said, if he were the cop investigating it, he wouldn't have taken Selena's and Jack's word for it. "Were you suspected of murdering your husband?"

"Yes. I was arrested, but the charges didn't stick. Jack made sure of it. I can't say I've been a fan of local law enforcement since. The detective investigating McGrath's death didn't seem like he cared who killed him. Jack said it was easy to simply arrest me and move on. The DA looked over the evidence Jack provided and dropped the charges. I was worried Jack might be arrested, but the detective, based on the DA's ruling, was quick to rule McGrath's death as accidental instead and closed the file."

Carter knew there were a lot of incompetent detectives out there. He would have at least pursued the possibility of bringing a case against Jack, depending on the evidence. Her experience with the police had been a negative one. He imagined that his being an ex-cop had been another black mark against him.

"It's late; we should go to bed," Selena mumbled the words against Carter's chest.

Carter lifted Selena with his good arm, carefully tossing her over his shoulder and making her laugh. He took her back to her bedroom and joined her in the bed. "You do know that this bed is amazing, and you won't be able to keep me out of it."

Selena heard the teasing words, but also the serious undertone. He was asking her for a commitment. She rolled onto her side, laying her head against his chest. "I like having you here. You can keep me warm."

Carter wrapped his arm around her, relieved she had acknowledged the beginning and the continuation of their affair. He waited until she fell asleep before he followed.

* * *

Selena's cell phone woke her shortly after sunrise. Beside her, Carter stirred but didn't wake up. She sat up and grabbed the phone. The text message was short, but oh so sweet.

Surprise! Baby girl, not boy. No name yet, as parents only had boy names picked out. Six pounds, nine ounces. Nineteen inches.

She sent a note back to Isabelle, telling her to congratulate the new parents. It was the perfect beginning to the day.

"What is it?" Carter's voice was gruff from sleep.

Selena set the phone down, a happy grin on her face. Carter's eyes were still closed. "Theo had a baby girl instead of a boy. It's funny because everyone thought Theo was going to be a boy before she was born and surprised everyone. Guess she started a family tradition."

"Mmm. I suppose you're going to want to see the baby." Carter yawned and stretched, but then settled back down. It was still early.

"I don't suppose that's a good idea, given what happened." Selena sat on the bed, her gaze on the buttons of the tuxedo shirt she had ended up sleeping in, her earlier smile now gone at the reminder that she wouldn't be able to see the baby.

Carter opened his eyes. He could see the sadness on her

face, but she was right. It wouldn't be a good idea. "When they feel up to it, you can video chat."

Selena sighed. She got up and went to the bathroom. She slid back under the covers while Carter took his turn, then came back to the bed.

"Are you going to get up?" Carter relaxed against the pillows. Her bed was really comfortable.

Selena glanced over at the man sprawled in her bed. She had a better idea, one guaranteed to banish her depression at not being able to see the baby. "Any more condoms in your jacket?"

That got Carter's eyes open. His body leapt to attention. "I have another one tucked in there, just in case."

Selena got out of bed and picked up his jacket. She found the second condom in the inside breast pocket. Clutching it in her hand, she climbed onto the bed, and then on top of Carter. As she did, Carter's hands slipped under the shirt. She felt his rough fingers caressing her breasts. It felt just as amazing as it had the night before. But she wanted to explore.

Carter's hands stilled as Selena bent forward and trailed kisses across his chest. He watched as she kissed and nipped her way down his body. She pressed her mouth against the skin of his lower belly, her hair brushing across his erection. Her fingers found him and explored. When her mouth lightly replaced her fingers, he reared up off the bed.

"Selena, my control isn't so great first thing in the morning." Carter gripped her shoulders, lifting her mouth and hands away from his aching flesh.

She simply smiled at him. She could feel the hardness of

him brushing against her body. "Okay, then it's my turn."

Carter watched as Selena slowly unbuttoned the tuxedo shirt, baring her body to him an inch at a time. His fingers clenched at his side. When she finally stripped the shirt off, he sat up so he could feast on her flesh. His mouth suckled and nipped at her breasts, much as she had to him. She lifted her arms above her head, arching herself, giving him full access to her body.

Selena suddenly dropped her arms to her side. "I want you to kiss me, Carter."

Amused and highly aroused by her demand, he took her mouth with his. She was not shy or hesitant. She cupped his jaw and devoured his mouth. The siren was in full control this morning. She pushed him back down onto his back, her mouth not leaving his. He couldn't remember any other woman making a feast of him the way Selena was.

Selena released his mouth. She wondered if her mouth was as red and swollen as his. She lifted her fingers to her lips. Then she realized she'd dropped the condom. She wriggled on top of him, trying to find it.

"You're killing me." Carter stilled the movement of her hips and took a moment to get a grip on his control.

She smiled triumphantly when she found it. She held it to him. "Would you like to do the honors?"

Carter took the condom from her and quickly rolled it on. He could tell she wanted to do it, but it would have been the end for him. Despite her inexperience, Selena was quickly learning her way around his body.

Selena's thighs tightened around Carter's. She settled her body lower on his but wasn't sure how to accomplish her mission. She looked up at Carter.

"Like this." Carter lifted her hips. He took her hand in his and had her guide him to the entrance of her body. "Now just ease yourself down slowly."

Selena felt a little pain as she brought him into her body, but it was nothing like what she had experienced last night. She did as he said and took him slowly. She let out a low moan when he was fully seated inside her.

"Now just rock your body." Carter gripped her waist, but she found the rhythm on her own. She was leaning over him now, her hands braced on his chest, and her body moving gracefully on his. He cupped her breasts as she moved on him, his eyes on hers.

Selena kept her eyes open, her breath panting in and out. She could see his eyes darkening as she brought them closer to the edge. She could feel his heart thundering under her palm. She could feel him dragging out of her and pushing back in as she moved. Incredibly she could feel him swelling inside her. She whimpered, a sound she never would have associated with herself. "Carter. Help me."

He suddenly sat up, pulling her legs tighter around him. He lifted his hips, thrusting deeper inside her. He felt her teeth nip his shoulder. Losing all control, he plunged even deeper, his body exploding into hers. He was barely aware of her soft cries in his ear, as she too went over the edge.

He fell back onto the bed, Selena collapsing on top of him. He could feel the sweat of their bodies mingling. He couldn't remember a time when he felt so drained from sex. Selena demanded everything he had to give and gave it back in return.

Selena lay completely spent on top of Carter. She kissed his chest, then tucked her arms around him. She sighed, and after a few minutes, fell asleep.

Carter saw her eyes close and felt a deep tenderness fill him. Still lodged inside her body, he followed her into sleep.

Chapter Eleven

Reality had to reassert itself, but Selena was not happy about it. Carter had woken her up from a deep sleep, playfully complaining that she was getting too heavy. He'd then made both of them get out of bed. Her thighs had been like rubber, and she'd had to lean on him as they made their way to her shower.

Now fully dressed, this time in a pair of cream-colored slacks and a pale pink blouse, she was running facial recognition on the man they had on camera. She figured her software would be faster than whatever software Detective Quinlan was using. She had asked McCray to email her the security files from the hotel. It had only taken him a short time to deliver them.

"Anything stand out?" Carter placed a hand on Selena's back as she leaned over her laptop.

"No. The tuxedos were plain. Even the cuff links were plain. No monogrammed cuff links or handkerchiefs. Nothing. He could have picked that tuxedo up at any shop in town."

"Do men really monogram their cuff links?" Carter pulled her hair to the side and placed a light kiss on the back of her neck.

She shivered but wasn't going to let herself be distracted. "Yes, they do. I have my grandfather's cuff links and they're monogrammed. They were a gift from my grandmother. She gave them to him when she found out she was pregnant with their first child."

Carter kissed her again. "Shouldn't he have gotten her a gift, not the other way around?"

"Grandpa Powell wasn't keen on the idea of children. He was too focused on his budding antiquities business. So when Grandma Powell found out she was pregnant, she thought that if she gave him a present when she told him, he couldn't be too upset about it. And she was having twins, so she thought a pair of cuff links in honor of a pair of babies was suiting."

Carter's hands drifted to her shoulders, then down to her breasts. He could feel them swell through her clothes. "How did he take it?"

Selena looked up at him, incredulous that he was trying to have a conversation with her. Willing to play his game, she concentrated on her story instead of his hands. "The story goes he wore the cuff links on the day of his sons' birth. My father and his brother came out squalling, and Grandpa Powell fell in love with his sons."

Carter's fingers found their way inside her blouse. "That's a nice story."

"Grandpa and Grandma Powell were great. I still miss them. They died within a couple of weeks of each other. First Grandma, then Grandpa."

Selena gave up trying to have a rational conversation. She lifted her arms and wrapped them around Carter's neck. In turn, her breasts lifted higher, and Carter started tugging her blouse out of the waistband of her pants.

"Sorry to interrupt, but I thought you two would be working." Ellis stood outside the office door, extremely amused when Selena went bright crimson red and tried to straighten her blouse with Carter's hand inside it.

Carter untangled his fingers from Selena's blouse and stood in front of her so Ellis couldn't see her fastening her clothes. "Don't you knock?"

"Seriously? I've been her bodyguard for six years. I don't knock."

"Then learn how." Carter turned and sat on the edge of Selena's desk.

Ellis chuckled. "You two make any progress on the case?"

Selena scooted around Carter so she could see him. "Running the security footage now. Not much else to go on, but at least it's something."

"Have mercy." Ellis walked over and cupped Selena's chin.

She flinched but didn't move. The bruising on her face was much more prominent this morning. She had a bruise on her temple, opposite the cut. She had a darkening bruise on the side of her face where the large man had hit her in the face with his gun. The skin around her mouth, where the tape had been, was still irritated. He couldn't see it, but she had quite the goose egg on the right side of her head where she'd been hit the final time.

"I look a sight." Selena gently pulled her face from his hands.

Ellis tucked his hands in his pockets and gave Carter a fierce look. He knew Carter got the message when the man nodded slightly. This had better not happen again.

Ellis eased himself onto the couch. He probably shouldn't be out of bed, but he couldn't stand not being part of the investigation. He could lie on Selena's couch just as well as his bed. "So what progress have you made?"

Selena's computer dinged, and she shot him a triumphant smile. "Looks like I got a name."

Ellis didn't get up from the couch, but he watched as Carter settled himself beside Selena. Looked like Selena got what she wanted, and he wasn't talking about the name. He could see possessiveness in every line of Carter's body. He couldn't help but be happy for her. "Well?"

Selena read off the details. "Anders, Michael. Age forty-seven. Married with two children in high school. Currently self-employed. His business website says he's a handyman. A quick check of his bank account tells me he must be an awfully good handyman because he charges some hefty fees."

Carter leaned over her shoulder. "The site is very generic. Doesn't have contact information on it. It says referral only. Maybe I should get myself referred."

Selena looked up at Carter. She could see the cop he used to be. "I suppose that's one option. Probably wouldn't be too hard to hack his account and get an appointment. I could call Jack and see who he recommends."

Ellis commented from the couch. "Yeah, right. Like Carter's going to let you send in someone else. But you should call McCray. Get a couple of extra security guards here while Carter's away. Or if you'd rather, you could call Jack and get some of his men here."

Selena shot Wallace a dirty look, but she knew he had the right of it. She could tell by the look on Carter's face that he wasn't going to stand by and wait while someone else found this Anders fellow.

Selena saw Carter watching her, waiting to see what she would do. She gave in, but not gracefully. "It might take me a while to get into his accounts. And when I do, you have to be convincing. I'm guessing this guy is going to be extra careful after what happened at the hotel. But I think my time would be better spent tracking who paid him last than you trying to contact him."

Carter leaned over her shoulder. "You can keep doing that after you get me in. It's possible he doesn't know much about who hired him. If that's the case, you'll have to keep digging."

A slight snoring sound from the sofa had both of them turning. Selena shook her head. "I don't think he's going to be much help. You've got a couple of choices. You can call McCray and use one of our guys, but I think that might not be a good idea. Our main man knows a lot about me and those around me. I'd suggest calling Jack."

Carter shook his head. "I'm thinking I might call Detective Quinlan. He seems like a competent man, and it would be better if we did this with the law on our side. Cops don't usually like using civilians, but he might make an exception for me."

"Boy's club." Selena tapped a few keys in disgust.

"More like once a cop, always a cop. I thought I could shut it off when I quit. These past couple of weeks have proven I can't. And I can't be something I'm not, Selena. I'm not like those rich men you date. I care about loftier things than what car I drive and the toys I own."

Though there was a lot of truth in his words, they made her angry. "And I'm just another rich man's toy. I get it. I can't be something I'm not, either."

Carter wasn't sure how she had turned his words back on him and was bewildered when she stormed out of the office.

"You stuck your foot in your mouth on that one." Ellis rolled onto his side, trying to get comfortable.

Carter could only agree. "I'm not sure how to get it out without making it worse."

"Can't help you, man. I let her stay mad at me. She eventually needs me and comes back. We pretend it never happened. It can take a few days for her to get over her mad, though, and I'm guessing you aren't interested in sleeping alone tonight."

Carter cursed under his breath. He walked into the hall and listened. The house was quiet. He debated which direction he should head first. Figuring the music room was his best bet, he headed there first. He found Selena staring out the back window.

"Selena, I didn't mean that the way you took it." Carter closed the door behind him so they wouldn't disturb Ellis, who was likely already snoring on the couch.

Selena wrapped her arms around her waist, keeping her back to Carter. "No? It doesn't matter what you meant. People generally have a way of speaking the truth, even when they don't mean to."

Carter came to where Selena stood. He turned her to him, despite her struggling against him. In the end, he was a lot stronger than she was. When she refused to look at him, he tipped her chin. He dropped his hand, shocked by the tears on her cheeks. The look in her eyes cut away at his anger. And he felt like a jerk for having made her cry. Knowing her the way he did now, he knew he had hurt her with his careless words.

Selena wiped her fingers over her cheeks, angrier at herself for allowing him to reduce her to tears than she was at him. "Leave me alone, Carter."

"At least you haven't regressed to Sullivan again. I swear, Selena, I didn't mean you were a rich man's toy. I just meant I'm not the type of man you normally date."

Selena sniffled a bit, and some of the pain she'd felt at his words fell away at the sincerity in his eyes. "You're right about that. You're not like the men I date. But that isn't a bad thing. As far as those men were concerned, I was just one more possession. You aren't wrong about that. I guess I just didn't care what they thought because I didn't care about them."

Carter brushed the last of her tears from her cheeks. "What about me?"

Selena took a step back, not ready yet for his touch. "I care about you, Carter. I couldn't have gone to bed with you if I didn't. I could have wanted you; I could have kept lusting after you, but I wouldn't have allowed myself to have you. Despite what you might think, or what you think you want out of this relationship we've started, I never expected it. I don't know what to do about it. And honestly, I'm not sure where it will go. As you said, we're very different. I'm guessing I'm not like the women you date, any more than you're the type of man I date."

Carter let her retreat, but not far. "I care about you, too. And for the record, I haven't dated at all since the shooting. My old type didn't appeal to me anymore. And I don't know what I expect from this relationship, other than the usual. I expect it to be just you and me. I expect there will be good times. I expect to wake up in your bed in the morning. I expect we'll argue sometimes, as we're doing now. I expect you to stick around and fight with me, not run away from me. You're not the type to give up easily. And I don't want to make you cry."

Selena brushed the last of her tears away. "I can live with all that. And I'm not a crier."

"No, you're a fighter. I noticed that about you from the beginning. You didn't back down when you were mad at me. You told me off." Carter walked toward her and pulled her into his arms when she didn't retreat again.

Selena rested her head on his chest. "So now what?"

Carter rested his chin on the top of her head. "First, we stand here for a moment. Then we take a brief break and have lunch. Then we go back to work. You'll start digging on the computer, and I'll call Mac. If nothing else comes of the call, at least he'll know what we know."

Selena nodded and didn't pull away. He was right. They needed to take a moment. "I bet you were a good cop."

Carter rubbed his hands up and down her back. "I like to think so. I had convinced myself I couldn't be good at it anymore. I guess I just needed a break and time to adjust to what had happened."

Selena bit her lip, but couldn't stop the question, though she didn't want an answer to it. "Do you think you'll go back to being a cop?"

Her question gave him pause. Is that what he wanted? He realized the idea had been tickling his subconscious. He had been away for two years now, but he knew that after what he'd gone through protecting Selena, he could handle the physical demands. He had been a decorated detective and was on the fast track for promotion. "I don't know. I might."

It wasn't the answer she expected, but she understood his hesitation to say one way or the other. He said he might, but she knew, deep down, that he would. He was one of the good guys, and the world needed more of them. She tipped her face up to him, standing on her tiptoes so she could kiss him. She felt his fingers brush against her cheek as he returned the kiss.

Selena was the one who broke off the kiss. "Next step of your plan was lunch. We might as well go raid the fridge. I'm going to need energy to track this guy."

Carter let her go. "Right. Food. Just remember where we left off later tonight."

Selena blushed and left the music room. Carter followed.

As soon as they finished lunch, Carter called Detective Quinlan. From what Selena could hear from Carter's side of the conversation, the detective had gone for the idea. Three hours later it still irritated her that, had she called the detective, the idea would have been shot down. Law enforcement didn't take her seriously; again she just wasn't intimidating, which was why she either tipped them off anonymously, or she had Wallace do it.

Within an hour of the call, the detective, who insisted she

call him Mac, arrived. She couldn't help feeling a bit smug as he checked out the house. He seemed reluctantly impressed with her home, much as Carter had been when he first arrived.

"He took the bait. You have an appointment with him tomorrow night. I arranged it at a seedy club across town, but not so seedy that he might get suspicious." Selena rubbed her eyes. Fatigue weighed heavily on her.

Mac looked at the details of the meeting Selena had forwarded to him. "All right. I want you to get out of the system and leave the rest to me. I can't have you compromising the investigation."

Selena folded her hands across her chest and glared at the detective. "So it's okay if you use my computer skills to locate this guy, but then I'm supposed to just sit here and keep my delicate little hands out of it?"

Mac admired Selena's spirit. She wasn't happy that she was being left behind while he and her boyfriend chased the bad guys. But in the end, it was his job to keep her safe. "We have experience, you don't. And these men have already proven how dangerous they can be. It's better if they think the cops traced them, not a high-society babe with a brain. And certainly not by the one who is their main target. They almost killed you once, almost killed Wallace, and they got way too close a second time. So I repeat, stay out of it."

Ellis, who was still resting on Selena's couch, snickered at the society babe comment. "I'll make sure she stays out of trouble. The babe and I will keep the home fires burning."

Selena shook her head, but she felt a smile forming

despite herself. "All right, I'll get my electronic prints off your case. I have plenty of real work to do. I still have a business to run."

Carter didn't look up, but he felt the weight of her words. It was an unwelcome reminder of how different they were. Since they had become lovers, it had been easy to pretend Selena was a normal woman. But the reality was that she was the owner of one of the most profitable companies in the state of California, probably the country.

Carter stood and stretched. Selena looked ready to collapse. "There's nothing else we can do until tomorrow night, except lie low."

Mac rose from his spot on the oversized couch. "I'll meet you outside the bar tomorrow night, three hours before the meeting. That should give us enough time to set up surveillance before our man arrives. I'll have a couple of cops staking out the place tonight and tomorrow, in case our guy is the overly cautious type."

Carter walked Mac out. When he returned, Ellis was on his feet. "Need help getting home?"

Ellis shook his head. "My warden is waiting outside, about halfway between here and there. She'll get me back to bed."

Selena followed Wallace out. She could see Roxanne on the path between the two homes. She gave her a wave and shut the door behind him. She set the alarm.

Carter came up behind her, settling his hands on her shoulders. The dark circles under her eyes were more prominent than they had been earlier in the day. She had covered most of the bruises up with makeup before Mac had arrived. But no amount of makeup was going to mask the tension in her body.

Selena stood still while Carter rubbed her shoulders. "Promise me you'll be careful tomorrow."

Carter turned her, bringing their bodies flush. His lips captured hers in a heated kiss. Her body melted against him. He picked her up and carried her up the stairs to her bedroom. He didn't turn on the lights, as Selena had left a small lamp burning on the dresser. He set her on her feet and kissed her again, taking her arms and wrapping them around his neck.

It didn't escape her notice that he had not promised to be careful. She supposed it was a promise he couldn't make. Feeling a little bit desperate, she clung to him, deepening the kiss.

Carter only broke off the kiss long enough to strip both of them of their clothes. He settled Selena in the center of the bed. He kissed his way from her mouth to her breasts. She arched beneath the caresses, clutching the blanket beneath her. He continued kissing his way down her body until he reached his destination.

Selena's hips bucked off the bed when Carter found the core of her body with his tongue. She wasn't sure if she should be embarrassed by the intimate caress and beg him to stop, or if she should simply beg him for more of the bold touch. Selena's thighs dropped farther apart, her hands clutching his hair.

It only took a few moments before Carter felt Selena's body peak and release. Not finished with her yet, he climbed back up her body, kissing her stomach and breasts as he went. Selena's eyes were dazed with the pleasure he had given her. Crouching now between her legs, Carter lifted her hips, put on the condom he'd left on the bedside table, and slid into her with one quick thrust. Selena arched her back in response to the sudden invasion as Carter established a fast rhythm. Gripping her hips, he pulled her firmly against him, as if he could absorb her into his body. She once again climaxed beneath him. Carter bent to kiss her and followed her over the edge.

Selena lay completely limp beneath him. She couldn't imagine ever allowing any other man to touch her the way Carter did. She couldn't imagine ever wanting anyone else to. Not thinking beyond the moment, she heard herself tell him how she felt. "I love you, Carter."

Carter barely registered the words at first. His heart was still pounding in his chest, and he'd yet to catch his breath. Then he realized what she had said. He lifted himself off and away from her. He sat on the edge of the bed, unsure of what to say.

Selena tensed when Carter pulled away from her. Embarrassed by her words and by her nudity, she left the bed and pulled on a robe. "I'm sorry, I shouldn't have said that."

It wasn't the first time a woman had said those words to him. He'd even said them himself a couple of times, though he supposed he didn't mean them the way a man should when he said them. He turned back to see Selena belting her robe. Her hair shielded her face from him. He realized she meant them; that it wasn't just the heat of the moment.

Selena went to the dresser and switched off the lamp.

"We should probably get some sleep. You've got a long day tomorrow."

"Selena. Please come here." Carter spoke softly in the darkness of the bedroom.

Selena found herself obeying his command. She came and stood between his knees. His hands gripped her waist, holding her to him.

"We don't know each other well enough for you to love me. Things have been crazy, and you've been under a lot of stress. What we have is good, and it's easy to confuse what you're feeling."

He didn't believe her. It made her heart ache, but she understood why. Given the suddenness of their relationship and given that a few days ago he didn't even like her, possibly still didn't, he couldn't understand how she could love him.

When she didn't respond, he stripped her of the robe she had just put on and pulled her onto the bed. She rolled over to her side of the bed and kept her back to him. When he came up behind her and hugged her body to his, he was relieved she didn't protest.

The room was quiet for a time. Selena took a deep breath before she found her words. "You don't have to love me, Carter. But I'm not confused by what has happened between us. I'm not confusing gratitude or lust with love. And I won't say it again."

Carter held her tighter to him, feeling confused himself. He didn't know what he felt for her. He cared, certainly. He was invested in seeing her through this crisis. The sex was amazing. She was incredibly responsive. But he had to remember that before he touched her, she had been a virgin. She had a husband who tried to kill her. She dated men who didn't care about her, since they hadn't made it past her defenses. She might not think she was confusing love and lust, but he wasn't naïve. What they were experiencing together was not a normal relationship. Before he used those words himself, they needed to get to know each other under normal circumstances. And when he found out who tried to kill her, he was looking forward to a normal relationship between them. Maybe then he'd figure out if what he was feeling was love or just passing attraction.

Chapter Twelve

The next evening, Selena was pacing her office. "How long do you think it will be before we hear from them?"

Ellis was once again stretched out on Selena's sofa. "Probably not for a few hours. The meet isn't scheduled until nine, and it's only seven."

Selena glanced at the clock. Wallace was right. She dropped into her office chair, but she was rocking it back and forth, unable to be still. "He should at least have let me set up surveillance instead of relying on Detective Quinlan."

"Using the police's surveillance keeps the footage from being questioned should the case go to court." Ellis had been fielding questions like that one for the last hour.

"But what if he…"

Ellis interrupted. "He knows what he's doing. He'll be just fine. Why don't you do something useful?"

"I haven't been able to track Anders's accounts back to a name. There are a lot of shell companies out there being used to pay off men like Anders who will do anything for a buck. And you're supposed to be helping me, not lying there watching me work."

"The detective wants you to stay out of it. Carter wants you to stay out of it."

"I don't care what the detective thinks. And I especially don't care what Carter thinks." Selena stopped spinning her chair.

"Yeah, right. You're in love with the guy. That's what's got you in such a twist."

Selena thought about denying it, but Wallace knew her better than anyone else, even Carter. "Fine. I love him. I even told him, for all he cares."

That got Ellis's attention. "What did he say after your grand declaration?"

"That I'm confusing love and lust. He's got an answer for everything. Says we don't have enough in common, and that we haven't known each other long enough to have developed those kinds of feelings."

"So the guy's an idiot. But he's a guy, so you'll have to cut him some slack."

"What about you? You were in love with Lindsay. What happened? Why didn't you try to make it work?" Selena found herself asking, though she knew why they had broken up. But hearing his answers again was suddenly important.

"I wouldn't compare my relationship with Lindsay to yours with Carter. But the short answer is that I was a class A jerk. I loved her, but I didn't love her brother. I made her choose. She chose him, and I chose to break it off. I don't have very many regrets, but she's one of them. But I was young and stupid, and I didn't know what I was throwing away."

"I saw Lindsay at the ball. She said her brother got married." Selena came over and sat on the edge of the couch near Wallace's feet.

"I know. She told me in a handwritten invitation to her wedding."

"What? She didn't mention that when I talked to her." Selena couldn't help feeling guilty for what she had thought of doing by hiring Lindsay's masseur. It was a good thing Carter told her to keep out of it.

"I've kept tabs on her. I guess I've felt responsible for her, even though I left. She's always been vulnerable, and I didn't want to see her taken advantage of or hurt." Ellis closed his eyes, not wanting Selena to see the hurt that still lived inside him. It was faint after all these years, but it was still there.

"Are you going to go?" Selena laid her hand on Wallace's knee.

"I think I owe her that much. I haven't met the man she's marrying, but I did a check on him. He seems like a nice enough guy. He's deep into the Hollywood scene, which will make Lindsay happy. If she had her way, she'd have been a famous actress."

They were quiet for a while. Then Ellis opened his eyes again and saw the hurt on Selena's face. "Give him time. He's been through a lot in the past two years. He cares about you, Selena. You can see it when he looks at you. You're just different from what he's used to, and it might take him a little longer to get to where you are. Just be patient and be waiting when he does. Don't throw the relationship away because of pride."

Selena sighed, then got to her feet. "I have never been a patient person, but I suppose I can give it a try. He's worth it."

"Good. Now get back to work."

* * *

"What do you think the chances are that your girlfriend is sitting at home watching television?" Mac stretched and settled back against the driver's seat of his sedan.

Carter stretched his legs. They'd been sitting there for a couple of hours now. "Slim to none. If I know Selena, she's digging further into our guy's financials to see if she can trace his clients."

"That's what I figured. She seemed upset yesterday at being left out, and she doesn't strike me as the type to give in or follow orders."

Carter thought about that but didn't have to think very hard. "No, she's better at giving orders. She's threatened to fire me a few times since I became her bodyguard. But I'm not gotten rid of easily. She's so used to being the one in charge; she can't fathom letting someone else take the lead."

Mac took a bite of a candy bar he had stashed in the glove compartment. "I checked your service records. You were one heck of a good cop. Sorry you gave it up?"

Carter took the second candy bar Mac offered him. They were cops in the same city, but they had worked in different precincts. "Recently, yes. It wasn't easy to do. It's all I ever wanted to do. But I felt completely inadequate after the shooting. Thought I would put my partner in danger, and in turn, those we were trying to protect. So I quit. I thought I'd made peace with my decision. Then Ellis was shot, and I took out the shooter. I ended up being Selena's bodyguard. Feels a bit like old times. Selena asked me yesterday if I wanted to go back to being a cop. I told her maybe."

Mac tossed the wrapper in the garbage bag in the back. "I could put in a good word. We're on the lookout for some good men. We had one detective retire, and another moved out of state. You've got good instincts, and you didn't let a pretty face steer you off track."

And what a face, Carter thought. Carter's wrapper joined Mac's. "Yeah, but I wanted to. She wasn't happy when I left this afternoon. She is extremely adept at giving a man the cold shoulder. I won't be surprised if she kicks me out of her bed tonight. She barely acknowledged me when I left."

"Those are the breaks." Mac wasn't feeling sympathetic. He hadn't had much to do with the opposite sex since his wife cheated on him and took off last year. But he wouldn't mind seeing a pretty face like Selena's over the breakfast table once in a while. But that wasn't easy to do with two kids in the house.

Carter sat up straight. "Our guy just pulled in."

Mac nodded. He'd seen him pull up, too. "We'll let him get nice and comfy before I go in."

They had agreed that Mac would play the client. Carter knew Selena was right about that. These men most likely knew who he was. He watched the man enter the building while Mac spoke on the open comm line. Cops were lying in wait. There were two inside and another two outside. Anders wasn't getting away.

The idea was to get Anders to agree to a job. All Anders had to do was rough up Mac's make-believe girlfriend. Once they agreed on the job, the cops outside would grab

Anders on his way out, with Mac right behind him. They didn't want to risk Anders having a weapon and putting the bar's patrons in danger.

Carter kept the line open once Mac left the car. The deal started fine. Carter heard them agree on a price. Then Anders said he needed to use the john. A few seconds later, Mac's voice came over the line. "We've been made. He's going out the back."

Carter didn't wait. They had two cops sitting out front. Carter, who had slid into the driver's seat when Mac left, slammed the car into gear. He drove around the building, slamming the vehicle to a halt when he spotted Anders.

Carter jumped from the car, his weapon drawn. "Freeze, Anders."

The man stopped for a split second, then spun on his heel to run in the opposite direction. Mac tackled him from behind. The two cops from inside were right behind him.

Carter came over, weapon trained on the man Mac was handcuffing. "Nice tackle."

Mac gave him a big grin. "Thanks. You were just enough of a distraction."

Carter holstered the weapon. Anders, now in handcuffs, was hollering about a setup.

Mac shoved the man toward the front of the building, toward the squad car that was now waiting. "Then it's a good thing we're not here to arrest you for conspiracy to commit a crime."

Anders spit on Mac's shoe. "Yeah, then what are you arresting me for?"

Mac rubbed the spit off his shoe onto Anders's pants.

"Conspiracy to commit rape. Conspiracy to commit murder. Those two charges should keep us busy for the rest of the night."

Carter followed behind as Mac read Anders his rights. The man was around five-eight maybe. That meant he'd put Selena's attacker at five-eleven or so. Selena was so petite; any man over five-ten would seem tall to her.

Mac struggled to keep Anders under control. The man was determined to fight him all the way to the squad car. "Settle down."

Anders gave Carter a twisted grin. "So who was it I was attempting to rape and murder? I don't suppose it's a lady about five-two, reddish-blonde hair? Real sweet piece?"

Carter grabbed the man by the collar, spinning him around. He barely refrained from slamming the man against the squad car. "If you know what's good for you, you'll be really nice and cooperative when my friend here gets you into an interrogation room. You don't want me to come after you."

"I'm really scared." Anders went to spit again, but Carter grabbed his face and pinched his mouth closed.

Mac opened the door and got Anders into the vehicle. He slammed the door. "I'll call you in the morning. I have a feeling this guy is going to play this game all night."

Carter nodded. "Want me to drive you back to the station?"

"No, you keep my car. Go ahead and swap vehicles. My car can sit in the parking lot overnight. I'll have one of my men pick it up later." Mac saluted Carter and climbed into the squad car.

Carter drove the sedan to where he'd left Selena's SUV parked. It was only a little after ten. He imagined Ellis was passed out on the couch by now, and Selena would have her nose pressed to her laptop screen.

Carter drove back to Selena's mansion at a sedate pace. He often did his best thinking behind the wheel of a vehicle. Never mind that the vehicle he was driving tonight probably cost more than his house. But he couldn't stop thinking about Selena being the target. Who would want her dead? None of the black market antiquities dealers she helped put in prison knew she was the one who gathered the evidence against them. Her father was in prison. Her husband was dead. And he wasn't buying that a radical group was behind this. One radical member might have tried to kill her. But a group of people coming after her seemed too far-fetched.

He and Jack had dug into her father's past. Nothing there, other than the attempted murder six years ago, raised any red flags. Her father had only a few visitors, mostly his twin brother. The two men looked nothing alike, so it wasn't as if they had arrested the wrong man. Not to mention, the idea was so out in left field as to be ridiculous.

But who else? Her father wouldn't benefit from her death, since he was in prison. He and Jack had already run down the brother. He was squeaky clean. Seemed like there was one good twin and one evil twin. And as far as he and Jack could tell, the only reason his brother even visited at all was out of family duty. Carter didn't tell Selena, because family was a touchy subject for her, but he had also run down her sister and brother. He had even run down

Daniel. Again, nothing. The brother and sister were typical rich kids, spending more money than they had, but nothing popped up on the radar. Daniel was exactly as he seemed: a slightly eccentric young man trying to carve out a living.

Carter turned the corner and opened the security gate. He waited and watched until the gate was closed. No one had followed him, but he wasn't taking any more chances with Selena. He waved to the two security guards posted outside the house. They nodded in acknowledgment. The men would remain there until morning, just as a precaution.

He was just about to unlock the front door when it opened. Selena stood there, wearing a lightweight nightgown and robe. She stood to the side so he could enter.

"I take it tonight's mission was a success." Selena reset the alarm.

"We got him. He's in custody right now. Mac isn't expecting the interrogation to go easy, but the man knows exactly who he is doing business with."

Selena wrapped her arms around her waist. "And how do you know that?"

"Gut feeling. He was taunting both Mac and me. He knows."

Selena gripped her waist tighter. "So do I."

"What?" Carter removed his jacket and faced Selena.

"I don't know who he is, exactly. I traced a deposit into Anders's account from the day before I was attacked. The money came from an offshore account to a man named Clarence McCoy."

"Alias?" Carter tossed the jacket on a side table and took Selena's arm. He led her to her office.

"Definitely. I'm running a check to see if that name pops up anywhere else. This guy is clever; I'll give him that."

Carter took her in his arms. "Not as clever as you. I have faith."

Selena pulled away and went to sit behind her desk. "At this point, I don't, so I'm glad one of us does. I've been hitting dead ends everywhere I search. In the morning, I'm going to have Wallace start digging, at least until he gets tired."

Carter circled the room, then came to stand in front of the desk. "Speaking of which, where is he?"

"I helped him upstairs to a guest room. As comfortable as my couch is, he'll be more comfortable in a bed. I had Roxanne bring a few of his things over so he can get right to work when he wakes up."

Carter placed his hands on the desk, leaning over so he could see her eyes. "How ticked off are you?"

Selena closed her eyes. "I'm not ticked off. I'm scared."

"There is nothing to worry about. I'm here, and there are two guards outside your front door. No one will get near you."

Selena gave him a sad laugh. "It's funny really. I should be scared that there is a madman out there trying to kill me. I should be scared because that man has come close to me, close enough to touch. He's determined, he knows where I live, and he knows everyone around me. He could so easily get to me through my friends if he wanted to."

"John and Jack will protect your friends. You can count on it. Ellis is as safe as you are behind these walls." Carter straightened.

"And what of you? Who's going to protect you? You went out tonight to catch a man willing to let another man kill me." Selena dropped her gaze, unable to look at him. "I know I said I wouldn't say it again, and I won't. But I don't think I could live with myself if something happens to you because of me."

Carter thought of her words of love. He could see tears in her eyes, tears for him. Whatever it was she did feel, she felt it deeply. He came around her desk and lifted her into his arms. She clutched at him, her face pressed against his chest. He sat in her chair, holding her to him. "I don't plan on anything happening to me either. I plan to stick around after we catch the man behind all this. When I do, we can see where this goes."

Selena unbuttoned a couple of the buttons on Carter's shirt and slipped her hand inside. "And where do you think this will go?"

"I'm not sure yet, Selena. But when I said I cared about you, I meant it. I can't remember feeling this way about any other woman before. For now, it's enough for me."

Selena supposed it was enough for her, at least for now. She relaxed in his arms. Caring could become so much more, and that was what she was betting on.

Carter leaned back. "You seriously have the most comfortable furniture."

Selena laughed against Carter's chest. "Sturdy, too. I've never made love in my office before."

Carter's hand slipped under the hem of Selena's nightgown, and he pulled a condom out of his back pocket. "Well then, I think I can fix that."

Selena was startled when Carter lifted her and sat her on the edge of her desk. She blindly shoved her laptop to the side. Carter stepped between her thighs, finding her bare flesh with his fingers. Her entire body shuddered, and she melted around his fingers.

Carter swore and sucked in a breath when Selena's fingers opened up the front of his jeans and found his eager flesh with her fingers.

Kissing her deeply, Carter shifted her so she could lean back on the desk. He sank into her, bending to cover her mouth with his so that her soft cries wouldn't be heard should Ellis come calling. Afterward, Carter carried a limp Selena to her bedroom, where he stripped them both and held her while they slept.

* * *

At dawn, Carter left Selena sleeping and went to find her laptop. He wanted to go over some of the files. Around seven, he got a phone call from Mac.

"Does Selena have a will?" Mac looked at the man in interrogation through the two-way mirror.

"No, I asked her who would stand to inherit should she die. She just shrugged and said she planned to leave everything to Daniel but hadn't gotten around to making it official. She said she wanted to wait until he was a little older. Otherwise, she said her family would fight over her possessions."

Mac was quiet for a moment. "Let's suppose that the shares she inherited could only be inherited by someone on her father's side. Or say they had to go to an existing shareholder. What would that mean for Selena's half of the business?"

Carter opened up an email and started typing. "If the shares had to go to someone on her father's side of the family, her father and his brother would inherit her shares. If only another shareholder could inherit them, then her father would inherit her half. He is the only shareholder besides Selena."

"Do me a favor and find out from Selena how the business charter is written. She and her father signed legal documents to protect their share of the company when Selena married Carter McGrath."

Carter stopped typing. "How do you know about Selena's marriage?"

"My friend Anders started getting chatty earlier this morning. He mentioned Selena's marriage."

That got Carter's attention. "According to Selena, the marriage never happened. If you try looking for evidence that it took place, you won't find it."

Mac heard what he wasn't saying. "So what you're saying is that I won't find a record of a wedding. So then how would a low-life gun-for-hire like Anders know about it?"

Carter didn't like this new twist at all. "You need to find out because Selena and her father are the only two people alive who know there even was a wedding."

"What about the business merger? Is there a record of that? It may mention a wedding. That could be how Anders knows about it. What I'm getting at is, I need a motive.

Who benefits if Selena dies? Or is this just about revenge, and if so, why? I know Jack, and if he couldn't dig it up, then I'd just be wasting my time if I tried."

"I'll have to ask Selena about the merger. There could very well be something in it that mentions a wedding. Selena told me the night she told me about her ex that the agreement didn't say how long she had to stay married, so I think it's a good bet it's at least hinted at, if not clearly spelled out. And her father may have a copy of the agreement somewhere. I can see if he has a safe deposit box or a storage unit of some kind."

"All right, get back to me. Anders hasn't said anything incriminating yet, but he also hasn't asked for a lawyer. We have him on film, and it's enough to get a warrant to search his home. Once I have that, I'll be sending a team to toss his house and seize his records."

"What about his wife? She clueless or complicit?" Carter gazed up at the ceiling, thinking of Selena.

"Not sure. Her husband didn't come home last night, and she hasn't filed a missing person report yet. And Anders didn't ask to make a phone call. It's hard to say."

"All right. I'll see what I can dig up on my end. I'll text you if I find anything." Carter hung up the phone.

"What about the merger?" Selena stood in the doorway so she wouldn't disturb Carter's phone call.

"Mac isn't having much luck interrogating Anders. He's having too much fun playing games. Mac did say he mentioned your marriage, which raises some questions."

Selena took a sip of her coffee and contemplated what he said. "No one should know about the wedding. How does he know? As far as the law is concerned, it never happened."

"What about the merger? You said the merger contract didn't state how long the marriage had to last. So it must at least hint at marriage. And Mac wants to know who would inherit your shares if you were to die today."

Selena shivered despite the heat from the coffee. She had a chill that wouldn't go away. "If I died today, I guess my father would inherit the shares. The company charter distributes shares to holders only if there is no will. It was a precaution in case one of the shareholders was unworthy to hold more shares in the event of a shareholder's death. I inherited my mother's shares because she left them to her three children, and my brother and sister didn't want them. Now there is just me and my dad. If I were to die, and then my father, then the shares would be split among the family members left of the last shareholder."

"So without a will, your father would inherit. What about the marriage and the merger?"

Selena came around to the computer. "I can pull it up. I have it on file. I didn't think to destroy it when I destroyed my marriage license. But I can tell you that it mentions marriage. In the event of a divorce, the company stays merged."

Carter started reading the document Selena pulled up. "So there was no marriage, so that means there was no merger. Who inherited your husband's share of the business?"

Selena considered what he was saying. "My father and I split the shares since the company was technically merged at the time. But with there being no merger without proof of marriage, then I guess we unrightfully inherited his part of the business. As far as I know, McGrath had no living family members, so I suppose the government would have seized his assets. I suppose there is no one out there to dispute my and my father's claim."

Carter wasn't particularly worried. Given Ellis's computer skills, he had no doubt he could manufacture a contract stating ownership without marriage. Though certainly not legal or ethical, given what Selena went through, Carter wouldn't lose sleep over it.

"So the next question is, who would have access to the merger contract?" Carter closed the file. He didn't need to read the details; he'd seen enough to answer Mac's questions.

"I do. My father might have a copy somewhere. And then McGrath would have had one. I don't know what would have happened to it. When I emptied our apartment, I didn't find much in the way of paperwork. He kept everything on the computer."

Carter nodded and sent a text to Mac. "I'm not sure where Mac is going with his line of questioning, but I think right now he's just fishing."

"That's all I've been doing. Once Wallace wakes up, he's going to give it a try. We've got another alias to track, and he's a better tracker than I am."

"Sounds like a plan. I'll go see if he's awake yet." Carter kissed Selena briefly, then left the room.

Selena listened to the sound of Carter's footsteps on the stairs. She could feel they were closing in. She rubbed her arms, trying to warm herself.

Chapter Thirteen

Carter hung up the phone. "Anders finally gave Mac a name and an address, and it wasn't Clarence McCoy. He said the man's name is Cedric Marin."

Ellis lifted his gaze from the computer he'd been staring at for the past two hours. "It's about time. He has to know the police have him cold on the two attempt charges. He should have been scrambling to make a deal hours ago."

"I'm going with him." Carter grabbed his jacket and the gun holster he had hidden beneath the jacket so Selena wouldn't see it.

Selena knew she couldn't talk him out of it but felt the need to try. "You're a civilian, not a cop."

Ellis piped in. "Once a cop, always a cop."

Carter ignored the quip and kept his eyes on Selena's. "It will only be a technicality for a little while longer."

Selena swallowed the lump in her throat. She had known he would go back to being a cop. She hadn't believed his maybe. "Then I'll just say, be careful."

Carter crossed to her. Ignoring their audience, he pulled Selena into his arms and kissed her. When she didn't resist, he deepened the kiss, hoping his kiss would act like a brand. She was his, and as soon as this mess was over, he'd figure out what he was going to do about it.

Carter released her as suddenly as he'd grabbed her. "I'll

be back; I promise."

Selena touched her lips, trying to hold the heat of his touch. Sighing again, she went back to her laptop. "We've got to be missing something here."

"I'll start a list of what we know. Somehow, someway, these men are connected." Ellis plugged his laptop into Selena's television so they could both see the screen.

An hour later, Selena was still staring at the list. "Cameron Malloy. Clarence McCoy. Michael Anders. Cedric Marin. Business mergers. Shell accounts. Aliases. Radical groups. Which one of these things is not like the others?"

Ellis grinned at the old Sesame Street reference. "I think we can eliminate radical groups. Mallory might have been a radical, but he wasn't working for a group."

"No, he was working for McCoy, or Marin, or whoever he is." Something was tugging at her brain, but it wouldn't quite take shape.

"And we're pretty sure Malloy was working for McCoy or Marin, not the other way around. Our main guy is staying in the background." Ellis removed "radical group" from the list.

"He only stayed in the background until he attacked me. And he knew almost everything about me and those around me." Something still nagged at her.

"Besides Carter and me, who else would know these things about you?"

Selena shrugged. "I suppose anyone could if they wanted to spend the time and money to investigate me. My father is the only person who might benefit from my death."

Ellis typed the words "benefits" and "death" on the screen.

Selena gasped. "Clarence McCoy, Cameron Mallory, and Cedric Marin. The initials C.M."

Ellis realized where she was going with this. "Carter McGrath."

Selena rose and started pacing. "What if he's not dead? The body was the right height, weight, and size, but it was burned beyond recognition. We assumed it was him. An autopsy might have been inconclusive."

"They would have had dental records, Selena. Though I suppose there are ways around that." Ellis realized he was starting to buy into her theory. It made sense.

Selena tried to recall what she knew about the records of his death. "The teeth were damaged in the crash. The teeth and jaw fit that of a man of his description. His identification was found in part of the plane that didn't burn. The coroner pronounced a positive identification. But if I'm right, and McGrath is still alive, he thinks we're still married. And if he were alive, he thinks he still has a third of the shares, instead of just ownership of his original business. He would then think my father has his third, and that my third would be split between the two of them."

"Selena, there is no proof McGrath is alive. If he is, who was the man in the plane? And if he is, why would he wait so long?"

She couldn't answer the question about the man in the plane, but she could answer the other question. "The company hadn't been doing very well up until last year. Things were still a bit shaky financially. My father had run the business so far into the ground that it's taken me these past six years to finally get the company in the black."

Ellis's mouth hung open for a second. "Just now in the black? You have this huge house, all this stuff, and the business has been in the red?"

"The money that went into the house and my 'stuff' was from personal investments I made from the money my grandfather left me. I opted not to put my own money into the business in case I failed to revive it. My grandfather left my father and mother the business, which had been in great shape. He left his house and his personal belongings to his other son, which amounted to a lot of money if sold. But he left all actual cash and investments to me. He was afraid I would become a starving artist."

"How could I know you for all these years and not know that?" Ellis just shook his head.

"Talking about money is considered crass. I also get a nice salary from my job as owner, which I've also invested." Selena used Wallace's laptop to pull up the company's financials.

Ellis glanced over the statement. "Looks like you reinvested a lot of money back into the company and its people. They were wise investments. Even after all these years, you still amaze me on occasion."

"Thanks. And those investments now put the company on solid footing. So much so that, should I die, the company would survive for a time without me. A new owner could come in and take over without having to put in much effort."

Ellis compiled all the information into a single file. "If your theory is correct, we can see if we can track McGrath."

Selena picked up the phone and tried to call Carter.

There was no answer. She waited ten minutes and tried again without any luck. She tried Mac's number. Nothing. "I'm going to go to the police department and see if they can find them. They need to know who they're dealing with."

Ellis was too weak to stop her, so he tried to reason with her. "Selena, that's a dumb idea. They didn't go in alone. They'll find him."

"But what if it's just another decoy? You should keep searching the files and see if you can find McGrath. I'll be safe between here and the station." Selena ignored Wallace and grabbed her jacket and keys. She climbed behind the wheel of her Mercedes and took off to the station.

Ellis cursed from the couch but did as he was told. The best way to help her was to find McGrath, assuming he was alive. Twenty minutes later, he found proof.

* * *

"We're on a wild goose chase." Carter looked around the house of Cedric Marin. It didn't look as if anyone had lived there in a long time.

Mac could only agree. "There's nothing here. I'll have the techs dust for prints, but I don't think we're going to find anything."

"We should head back." Carter pulled out his phone. Selena had tried to call him. He dialed her back, but she didn't answer. He tried again; no answer.

"What is it?" Mac opened the car door and waited while Carter checked his phone.

"Selena's not picking up." Carter dialed Ellis. The man

answered on the first ring. "Where's Selena?"

"She took off to the station to see if she could find you or Mac. We did some digging. It's McGrath. I'm emailing you the file now."

Carter hung up and opened the email. Carter cursed out loud. "They finally traced the money back to her dead husband."

Mac leaned against the car. "How can that be?"

"He's not dead. Selena went to the station to find us."

It was Mac's turn to curse. "Which means she's out without protection."

Carter hopped in the car. Mac drove at top speed back to the station. When they arrived, there was no sign of her.

"Track her cell. She wouldn't have left home without it." Carter followed Mac while he pulled up the program to track her cell. "Her phone is off."

"There's no way she shut that off on her own." Carter felt real fear in his gut. It was so strong he couldn't think straight. McGrath must have her.

* * *

Selena woke to a pounding headache. She tried to move, but her arms and legs were bound. She suddenly remembered what happened. She had left her house to go to the police station. She remembered getting out of her vehicle. Before she could get near the entrance, a man had come up behind her.

"Hello, darling. I see you're finally awake." McGrath glanced into the backseat of the car where he had tossed her.

He was driving her car down the interstate, keeping an eye out for any sign of the police. So far, he had seen nothing.

"We know it was you." Selena struggled against the tape.

"You always were too smart for your own good. But I didn't make it too hard for you to find me. I wanted you to know I finally won our little game. You should have died like a good girl, but you just had to be difficult." McGrath pulled onto another main highway and headed further north.

"I'm not the only one who knows." Selena looked out the window to see if anything looked familiar.

"You mean your boyfriend, Sullivan? Or your bulldog, Wallace? Neither of them has proof."

Selena tried to keep the panic at bay. "That's what you think. You shouldn't have brought Michael Anders with you to the hotel. He was easy to track, and he's spilling his guts to Detective Macaulay Quinlan. Why don't you go and see for yourself?"

McGrath turned to look at her face, but he couldn't tell if she was lying. "Even if that were true, who would believe him?"

"What do you think is going to happen? You kill me, then come back from the dead? If you were alive, you would be wanted for attempted murder. My attempted murder." Selena looked back out the window. She saw nothing but light poles. She was pretty sure they were still on the highway.

"On the contrary, coming back from the dead is exactly what I plan to do. See, my wife and her boyfriend, Jack Warner, tried to murder me. Jack sabotaged my plane.

Unfortunately, my copilot was the one who died. I realized I had to hide, or else my wife and her boyfriend would come after me. When you die in a tragic accident, I will come out of hiding. I'll have plenty of evidence to support my side of the story. With your death, I can inherit my wife's shares of our antiquities business."

Selena was starting to panic. "My father will still own half. What about him?"

"Death in prison is easy if you have the cash. With you dead, I'll have plenty of cash. And I imagine while he's still alive, he'll be happy to see you die and him inheriting half your shares. Then he'll be dead, and I'll have what should have been mine six years ago."

Selena kept trying to loosen the tape, but it wouldn't budge. She closed her eyes against the tears forming. She could only pray Carter would find her before it was too late.

* * *

Carter paced the small office space. His mind had completely shut down. "So now what do we do? We can't trace her phone."

Mac pulled up a different program. "Does she have roadside assistance or GPS in her car? The officers checked, and her Mercedes is not in the parking lot. We can trace her vehicle."

Carter stopped pacing. "Her car has all the bells and whistles. Nothing but top-of-the-line for Selena."

It only took Mac a minute to pull up the vehicle's information so he could track the car. "There. He's headed north on the highway. Traffic is heavy this time of day. We may be able to catch him."

Mac and Carter headed for the squad car. The large SUV would make good time on the highway with sirens blaring. Carter called Ellis and relayed the information. Just in case something happened to the police equipment, he wanted Ellis tracking her.

Carter watched the screen and saw McGrath pull off the highway onto a county road. Thirty minutes later, the vehicle stopped in a rural part of the county. They were only ten minutes away. With his heart pounding, Carter prayed McGrath kept her alive long enough for them to catch up.

* * *

McGrath shoved Selena through the doorway of the farmhouse. "The police will find that this house belongs to you. A little hideaway for when the stress of your life gets to be too much. Unfortunately for you, the house has some very faulty wiring. You'll be torched while sleeping."

Selena realized he wasn't planning to wait to murder her until dark when normal people would be asleep. But it was already after eight o'clock, and who was to say she didn't turn in early?

"Up the stairs, darling. It's time for bed." McGrath shoved her with the barrel of the gun he held.

Selena stumbled as she reached the top of the stairs. He then shoved her into a bedroom. "You won't get away with this. No one will believe you."

"No, why is that? You ran off into hiding, unable to deal with the stress of all that has happened in the past few weeks."

Selena fell onto the bed when he gave her one final shove. "There's just one problem with your grand plan."

McGrath stripped off his jacket. "And what exactly is that?"

Selena paled as he started unbuttoning his shirt. She blurted out the words, "We're not married."

McGrath stopped removing his shirt. "I was there, remember. We had a nice little ceremony at your father's house."

Selena came up to her knees. "That's where you're wrong. There is no proof of a ceremony. You won't find any record of our wedding. I erased it."

McGrath came up to her and grabbed her chin roughly in his hands. "What do you mean, there's no record? We filed those papers. We are married."

"You and my father underestimated me time and again. You being dead wasn't enough. I wanted you eradicated from my life. I learned some fancy computer skills after you were gone. It's amazing what one can do with the right knowledge and equipment."

McGrath shoved her onto her back. "The judge is proof. Your father is proof."

Selena tried to calm her breathing as McGrath reached for the snap of his jeans. "The judge died last year. I went to his funeral. And my father is a convicted criminal. Who will the courts believe? With no proof, the business goes to my father. And I can say with some sincerity that he isn't going to give the business to you."

McGrath shouted in rage. He slapped Selena across the face, then again. He grabbed her blouse, ripping it down the middle. "You're lying. There's no way you can have erased our wedding. I will have you, and I will have the business."

"Make one more move toward her and I'll blow your head off." Carter came into the room, circling the space so he could see Selena.

McGrath took a step back, the gun in his hand pointing at Selena. "Well, well, if it isn't the boyfriend. Carter, isn't it? My wife seems to have a thing for men named Carter. I think I'll have to break her of the habit."

"Drop the gun. There's no getting out of this mess." Carter purposefully kept his eyes off Selena and on McGrath.

"That's where you're wrong. See, I have this feeling you aren't going to do anything to put my wife in danger. And if you don't drop your weapon, I promise you she is in danger."

Carter saw his finger tighten on the trigger. "All right. I'll put my weapon down, and you can walk out of here."

"I don't think so." McGrath turned to point the gun at Carter. Grinning, he squeezed the trigger.

Several shots were fired, and in a moment, McGrath lay on the floor, two bullets in his chest.

Mac came through the door, his weapon still trained on McGrath. "Are you hit?"

Carter rushed to Selena's side. He pulled her into his arms. "Are you all right?"

Selena lifted her taped arms around Carter's neck. "I'm okay. Are you okay?"

"I'm fine. Bullet missed, thanks to Mac." Carter kissed her, hugged him to her, then kissed her again.

"Looks like our friend here is still alive." Mac cuffed McGrath and knocked his weapon across the room.

Carter lifted Selena off the bed, her bound arms still around his neck. "Too bad. Guess we'll have to call an ambulance."

"Take her outside. Have Slater put in the call." Mac took the bed sheets and sliced them up with the knife he kept in his back pocket.

Carter pulled a knife out of his pocket and slowly cut the tape around Selena's wrists after he unwound them from around his neck. He could see tears streaming down her cheeks, stress from the ordeal catching up with her.

"I was worried I'd never see you again." Once the tape was cut off, she threw herself back into Carter's arms. She felt him slip an arm under her legs as he carried her out of the house.

"Trust me when I say I won't be going anywhere. I've never been so scared in my entire life." Carter walked past Detective Slater, one of the officers who had followed him and Mac up here.

"I love you, Carter. You may not love me, but I swear I won't ever let you go." Selena buried her face in his neck.

"You told me you weren't going to tell me again." Carter smiled at her words.

"I've never been very good at subtlety. And I'm not a very good liar. So long as you hang around, you'll have to learn to live with the words." Selena pulled back so she could see his face.

"No, I don't suppose you are good at subtlety or lying. I'd like to say I'm not good at those things, but I was an undercover cop, so I'd be lying. I can say truthfully that I have never been so scared in my entire life. I was so scared I couldn't think straight. That kind of fear makes you realize some very basic truths. And the most important truth is that I love you." Carter said the words with no hesitation.

Selena cried, but they were happy tears. "I can't say that I'm happy it took my being kidnapped for you to realize you love me, but I'll take it."

Carter cupped her face, careful of the new bruises forming. He kissed her tenderly, reverently. And no matter how different they might be, or how much money she had, he would be wherever she was. Some truths can't be denied.

Epilogue

"Never thought I'd see the day." Ellis was sipping a glass of champagne, watching the happy couple share their first dance as husband and wife. He could see tears in Selena's eyes, even with the distance between them. She'd written the beautiful, haunting song the couple was dancing to as a gift to her husband.

Jack took a large swallow of his beer. Theo and their daughter, Patricia, were across the room talking to Isabelle and John. "Can't say that I did either. I never thought she'd let her guard down long enough to fall in love."

"I knew she had a thing for him, but it's still a shame it took me getting shot to bring them together." Ellis couldn't help but smile, despite the fact that his body still hurt from the healing wounds.

"What was surprising was how quickly the two arranged the wedding. It's only been three weeks since McGrath was arrested." Jack set his beer down, feeling pleasantly buzzed. He was pretty sure the lack of sleep from having an infant in the house was making the beer go straight to his head.

"Selena wanted to have a real wedding. Carter didn't want to wait as long as a formal wedding would take. But Selena's got enough money that she was able to pull this off quickly."

Jack tipped his head so he could see Theo better. "So

what about you, Ellis? Ready to tie the knot?"

Ellis looked over at Lindsay, who was there with her fiancé. "I'm not ready yet. Never say never, and all that."

"I hear that. Theo took me by surprise, but I knew I wanted her. It was just a matter of convincing her that she wanted me. But it didn't take much persuasion." There was heat in Jack's eyes as he gazed at his wife. Her figure was fuller since she'd given birth, and he really liked it. Soon he'd be able to do something about it.

Ellis looked away from Lindsay and what he couldn't have. He'd burned that bridge years ago. He doubted he'd find another woman like her. His gaze crossed the room and settled on a different woman. His reaction to this one was strong. "Who invited her?"

Jack followed Ellis's gaze. "You mean Olivia?"

"Yeah, I mean Olivia."

Jack shrugged. "Needed a little extra security at this party. She volunteered. She's getting her investigator's license, and I figured a little guard duty would wet her feet. Get her out from behind her computer."

Ellis scowled. Olivia worked for Jack. The woman got on his last nerve. She seemed to think she was smarter than him. And she had taken an instant dislike to him when they'd met last year on a collaboration they'd done for Selena. Selena wanted to hire her permanently, but Olivia had declined. And she'd declined any further assignments through Jack. By the time the job had ended, Ellis had been glad to see her go.

"The woman is only five-six. She's too small to be a bodyguard. Keep her at her desk. It's where she belongs."

Ellis took a large swallow of his champagne and pulled his gaze away from the sexy length of her legs. In her high heels, she looked to be all leg.

Jack just laughed. "Just keep fighting it."

Ellis, ignoring Jack's comment, simply turned his back on her, but not before Olivia caught him watching her.

Both men looked back at the couple. The pair was hard to miss. Selena wore a creamy white wedding gown, one that hugged the curves of her body. She'd opted not to wear a veil, and the lights shone on the flowers she had woven in her hair. Carter had opted to wear the tux Selena had bought for him. Carter claimed to have a special fondness for the tux. When the dance ended, the newlywed couple came to the table to greet their friends.

Selena came up to Ellis and kissed him on the cheek. "What are you going to do while we're away?"

Ellis kissed her cheek back but didn't get up from his seat. "Rest and recuperate. Maybe I'll find myself a new nurse, a sexy blonde who will cater to my every whim."

Carter lightly punched Ellis's shoulder. "As long as you keep your hands off my sexy blonde, we'll be fine."

Ellis laughed, but when his gaze shifted back to Olivia, who just happened to be a sexy blonde, he scowled.

The party continued with good food, good wine, and plain beer for Jack. Carter and Selena made their rounds and said their goodbyes to their friends. When it was time to leave, they snuck out the back, with only John and Isabelle, Jack and Theo, and Ellis to see them off.

Carter pulled Selena onto his lap while they rode in the back of their rented limousine. They would spend a night in a luxury suite before hopping on a plane in the morning to go spend the next two weeks lying on white sand beaches, drinking fruity cocktails, and making love as often as possible.

Selena rested her head on her new husband's chest. "Two weeks of nothing but you and me."

"Mmm. Heaven." Carter kissed the top of her head, then tipped it up so he could savor her mouth.

There would be a lot of changes when they returned. Carter had already been hired at the precinct Mac worked at. It seemed odd, but it felt right to be a cop again. Selena had been nervous but supportive of his decision. She understood the importance of law and order, so she applauded his decision. She said that as long as he promised to come home to her every night, she could live with it.

Things would change for Selena, too. Carter had tried to talk her into giving up the antiquities business and following her passion for music. She'd told him that she had a responsibility to the people who worked for her and to the memory of her grandfather. However, because she didn't need a personal bodyguard anymore and because Ellis knew the business as well as she did, she was promoting him. Once he was fully recuperated, Ellis would take on a new role as vice president, a position that hadn't existed before.

Selena pulled away from the drugging kiss. "I almost forgot. I got you a present."

Carter didn't release her. Instead of kissing her, his hand slid under the hem of her dress. His hands slid higher, finding the bare skin over her garters. The feel of that soft skin made his body shudder with desire. It was going to be a long ride to the hotel.

Selena pulled a small jeweler's box out of the small purse she'd tossed on the seat. She flipped open the box to reveal a pair of gold cuff links. "Don't panic; I'm not pregnant."

Carter looked into her eyes, then back down at the gift. There was something different about the cuffs. "It would be okay if you were, but I'd like to have you to myself for a little while before we take that step."

Selena took a cuff link out of the box. She undid the plain one on the cuff of his right arm. "These are my grandfather's. But I wanted you to have a pair with your initials. I had the jeweler make a new engraved piece designed to fit over the top of his."

Incredibly moved by the gesture, Carter took the second cuff link out of the box. He could see where a disk of gold hooked over the top of the cuff. If he were to remove the disk, her grandfather's initials would be visible. He undid the other one and fastened the gift to his left cuff. He cupped Selena's chin, kissing her tenderly. Though desire still clawed at him, he couldn't think of a better way than the tender kiss to thank her for the beautiful gift.

Selena kissed him back, her mouth mobile on his. She wasn't embarrassed by the tears that wet her eyes. She pulled back for a moment and looked into her husband's eyes. "Say you love me, Carter."

Without hesitation, Carter kissed her back and poured all the feelings he had for her into the kiss. "I love you, Mrs. Sullivan."

Breathless, Selena curled contentedly in his lap as the

limo continued toward their destination. "I love you, Carter."

No other words were needed. And when the door closed behind them at the hotel, the words were once again shared, and then they expressed their love in the most elemental ways.

From The Author

I hope you enjoyed the third book in my series, The Heart's Way. All books in the series can be read alone, but I always think it's more fun to read them in order. Look for the next title in the series, Forever Love, available now. And if you missed out on the first two, you can get For Now and Always, and Ask Me To at your favorite retailer.

If you enjoyed the book and would like an email on my next release, please sign up for my newsletter @ elizabeth-castle.com/contact. Please be assured that your email will never be sold (I wouldn't want mine sold, so I wouldn't do that to someone else). You can also follow me on Facebook @ facebook.com/elizabethcastle.romanceauthor

Also, if you enjoyed this book, or any of my other titles, please consider leaving a rating at your favorite retailer, Goodreads and/or Bookbub. And if you have the time, a text review would be lovely. Indie authors rely on readers like you to tell others how much you enjoy their books.

Happy reading,

Elizabeth Castle

Books by Elizabeth Castle

Single Titles:
    Going Home
    This Kind Of Love
    Chasing Hope
    The Babe & The Librarian (novella)

The Heart's Way Series:
    For Now and Always
    Ask Me To
    Say You Love Me
    Forever Love

Bennett Family Series:
    This Time Love
    A Bride For David
(novella)

All Of Me Series:
    All Of My Days
    All Of My Nights

The Cantwell Quartet
Series:
    Falling Slowly
    Unraveled
    Hidden Away
    Entangled

Contemporary "Retro" Romance Series:
    Loving Jordan

Visit elizabeth-castle.com for newsletter sign up and up-to-date releases.